5 Ways to Kill Ramaa

AND OTHER STORIES

5 Ways to Kill Ramaa
AND OTHER STORIES

Devdas Chhotray

Translated by
Tapan K Panda

BLACK EAGLE BOOKS
Dublin, USA | Bhubaneswar, India

Black Eagle Books
USA address:
7464 Wisdom Lane
Dublin, OH 43016

India address:
E/312, Trident Galaxy, Kalinga Nagar,
Bhubaneswar-751003, Odisha, India

E-mail: info@blackeaglebooks.org
Website: www.blackeaglebooks.org

First International Edition Published by
Black Eagle Books, 2023

5 WAYS TO KILL RAMAA AND OTHER STORIES
by **Devdas Chhotray**
Translated by **Tapan K Panda**

Cover & Interior Design: Ezy's Publication

ISBN- 978-1-64560-363-4 (Paperback)
Library of Congress Control Number: 2023932413

Printed in the United States of America

Foreword

Adolescence has fascinated writers of fiction as it presents a dramatic transition from the innocence associated with childhood to the grim realities, complex betrayals, and compromises of adult life. Many works of fiction revolve around characters, who find themselves on the cusp of adulthood negotiating inarticulate longings and inchoate anxieties. As they begin to experience sexual awakening, they find themselves caught between explosive desire and oppressive conventions. Some, even while growing up, continue to inhabit the world of adolescence for it insulates them from the sorrows and disenchantmnents of adulthood. Such eternal adolescents, like Peter Pan, represent a protest against the world of adulthood and yet arouse our pity as they remain frozen in time.

Devdas Chhotray's stories and poems bring the world of adolescence vividly alive and portray its pain and ecstasy with unforgettable acuteness. The author deftly captures the moods of his young characters as they negotiate disappointments in love, feverishly plot fantastic schemes of revenge, and chronicle the painful process of growing up in a world that keeps thwarting their desires. The drama of coming of age unfolds in the evocative setting of small-town Cuttack, rapidly getting transformed by the emerging realities of post independence India. The lyrical intensity of the prose reenchants the drab little town, its dusty bylanes, and makes one feel nostalgic for a long-lost world. One response to these enthralling stories is a feeling of delicious melancholy.

Prof. Jatindra Kumar Nayak

Tantamount to Falsehood

About 50 years ago, when the most renowned apparel entrepreneur Jayanarayan Kedarnath displayed three mannequins attired in saree at his Cuttack's Nayasadak store for the first time, it created a sensation in the city and was mentioned in the newspaper. On my way back home riding a bicycle at 2 am from Keshu Betel Shop, I tried to avoid the back street as the dogs barked, I decided to return home through Nayasadak. I took notice of the three gorgeous mannequins draped in dazzling sarees firmly implanted in a glass case gleaming in the neon light similar to the gilded star firmament. I wondered if one of the mannequins, especially the midmost one, would have been viable, what would have happened? And a thousand recollections weaved their air-threads into woof—presumably if a perpetrator stationed as a mannequin would have led the police on a merry chase.

A year later, I mistook the guard standing in front of a palace in Berlin for an effigy. I was bewildered by the touch of his breath. His self-restraint could make him stand for hours together like a statuette with his assult rifle at the top of the significant official building in Europe. By then, the protagonist of my first story, 'Ramaa', had begun stirring my imagination. That afternoon, I indulged in a conjecture thought of Ramaa standing in place of the mannequin. Her figure was that of an undetermined form—but therein, I was critical.

Akshaya Mohanty introduced me to Ghalib and Jorge Luis Borges. Jorge Luis Borges was an Argentine writer and poet born in Buenos Aires in 1899. He was a gifted writer but never received the Nobel Prize in Literature, despite being one of the most emblematic literary voices in the world. He strongly influenced me through the genre-blending magic of his fictions and metafiction in his stories and poetry. He became completely blind at the age of 55 and could not read and write. Still, he mastered the world of literature through his imagination. He came up with poetic couplets recorded by his elderly mother which was first published in 'The Encounter', a magazine edited by Stephen Spender.

To date, though, I cannot precisely pronounce his exact name, but his book 'The Book of Sand' enchanted Akshaya Mohanty and me. Penguin published the book. There is sparseness to the prose in this collection's stories, a distancing, making them loom like myths or fables. They are certainly flavoured with the fantastic! One of my stories, 'Darpan' is influenced by his story 'The Other' from 'The Book of Sand.'

Waiting for a cup of coffee, I could wind up reading 'Coffee Pae Apekhya Kala Bele Duiti Gapa' twice before the coffee was served. According to a Bengali writer, a short story can be limited to the size of a postcard. These two short stories could fit into an inland letter, though not a postcard. One of my foreign friends read the story and asserted that she had never imagined so much malice lay bottled up within me. I kept quiet!

The experience of age, a figment of the imagination, and criticism of the so-called social norms and system within the monotony of life gave birth to the story 'Bhabantara.' 'Little Das MMS' is the amalgamation of contemporary language and a mysterious character.'Besa Posak' is a story based on a particular tailor and casual chit-chat. These three stories were published in *Katha*.

In 1995, while writing the script for 'Indradhanu Ra Chai (shadows of Rainbow)' to be featured in Cannes Film Festival, I protracted an interview scene. The story 'Interview' is the outcome of the conversation between Director Sushanta Mishra and the interviewee Sonia.

I wrote ' Bruta (The circle)' which found a place in the *Samukhya*, published by Psychology Professor Shri Radhanath Rath and his leftist companion Shri Rabi Das during my college career. The story ' Alice ra Bou (Mother of Alice)' is the creation of my immature mind, although it is close to my heart. The theme of this story is based on the mindset peculiar to a small city. This story was first published in *The Ka* and then in *The Galpa* and subsequently translated into Bengali. I still long for 'Alice Ra Bou.'

The story 'Jinisa (Material)' is very close to my heart. I was greatly influenced by a scene depicted in Bergman's film 'Seventh Seal' where the Count plays chess with Death. The anecdote, a tug of war between Life and Death, is the outcome of a tired and unconscious reality. Though the story 'Jinisa' is set in Cuttack, I notice that those who have a conscious perception of life will appreciate it. This story was published in *The Katha* and was much appreciated by the readers, which stimulated my creativity.

My dream is correlated to life. Vision and alertness are like a swing door through which my imagination and creativity move effortlessly. During one of his interviews, Graham Green once suggested, maintaining a dream diary for those who fantasize.' Dakhinatya' is a story that depicts a vivid dream I had seen during my stay in London. The characters in the story are the sequel of my dreamlike 'The Emperor' of 'Lal Macha (Red Fish)'.

When I narrate the story of my life, many listeners, specifically the Odia artist at London, Shri Prafulla Mohanty, commented, 'Debadas always lies.' I wonder if my individuality is the creation of my imagination or the act of transacting.

I acknowledge that my stories are tantamount to falsehood though it is perceptible at a certain point. Marquez said that a small lie in journalism could undermine a report, but an iota of truth emblazons the whole writing.

Devdas Chhotray

Translator's Note

Fantasy and prudence are like a swing door through which imagination and creativity move without any effort. Devdas Chhotray acknowledges that the stories are tantamount to falsehood though it is perceptible at a certain point.

'Five Ways to Kill Ramaa' is a uniuqe theme of the writer playfully toying with disparate ideas to kill Ramaa. The writer builds a castle in the air and conceptualizes five different ways of doing this. Since her childhood, he has known Ramaa. Then he had frequently visited Tiku, who is Ramaa's elder brother. She was a sloppy mess and had unkempt hair, which was covered with dandruff, and that's the reason why her hair was shaved frequently. In his childhood, Ramaa's living room became a place to enact the play where he and Ramaa acted like a couple and Tiku as a tutor. Ramaa draped herself with Kuni aunty's saree, decked herself up in jewels and had put vermilion on her forehead. He fantasized about Ramaa in the same attire when he was thirteen.

He still remembers when Ramaa wore a saree for the first time. She looked like a beautiful rose in her pink saree. She revealed her grandeur. She appeared like a bride, but he could never see her because, fifteen years after of this incident, she eloped with Bikas and solemnized her marriage in court.

Ramaa's attitude towards the writer was never favourable, but her first saree-draped matured figure transfigured him into a grown-up man.

In Bikas and Ramaa's story, the writer introduces the character Bikas. Bikas's personality enticed Ramaa, and she was put under a spell by his charm. Ramaa justified her action and, of course, succeeded in marrying Bikas. The writer was a scapegoat in this affair and witnessed their marriage. His bitterness for Bikas grew with time, and he always tried to find a way to spoil this prospering liaison.

'Why to Kill Ramaa' presents the writer's devilish vision of slaying Ramaa. In 'The First Attempt,' the writer spilled kerosene all over the floor and lit a fire. The glass case in which Ramaa was standing was engulfed with fire. The next day he turned the newspaper's pages, apprehending that the news might have been published but finally concluded that it was his dream but not the reality. In the second, third, fourth, and fifth attempts, the writer lists various strategies to kill Ramaa. These indicate his attitude and resentment for Ramaa.

'The Mirror' is influenced by the story 'The Other' from 'The Book of Sand'. The narrative reflects his own entity.

'Waiting for a Cup of Coffee' comprises two short stories that are meticulously written and concise. These two stories could fit into an inland letter, though not a postcard. One of his foreign friends read the story and asserted that she never knew so much malice lay within him.

The experience of age, a figment of the imagination, and the criticism of the so-called social norms and system within the monotony of life give birth to the story 'Reenvision. ' Little Das MMS' is the amalgamation of contemporary language and a mysterious character. 'The Attire' is a story based on a specific tailor and table talk. These three stories were published in *The Katha,* a monthly magazine in Odia.

'Interview' is a story of a befuddled interviewee. Devdas Chhotray, during his college career, wrote 'The Circle,' which was published in *The Samukhya* by the Psychology Professor Shri Radhanath Rath and his leftist companion Shri Rabi Das.' Alice's Mother' is the product of his immature mind. The theme of this story is based on the narrow world of a small city. This story was first published in *The Ka* and then in *The Galpa* and subsequently translated into Bengali.' Possessions' is a story that is very close to his heart. This story reflects on the possibilities of life after death.

The dream is correlated to life. Fiction and alertness are like a swing door through which imagination and creativity move without any effort. 'The Tale of a Southern City' is a story that depicts a vivid dream seen during his stay in London. The best part of this collection is the structure and form in which the author has crafted the stories. The anthology has the potential to establish a new style of story writing in Odia literature.

I translated these stories during the pandemic and couldn't complete the manuscript earlier. I thank beloved author, poet Sri Devdas Chhotray for permitting me to translate the Odisha Sahitya Academy Award winning collection *'Ramaaku Maaribara Panchoti Upaya'*. I wish to thank my dear friend and eminent writer Ms. Chirashree Indrasingh's daughter Madhur Singh Pradhan for reading the first draft and suggesting changes as a gen-Z reader. I couldn't have completed this project without the kind help and suggestions from Prof Jatindra Kumar Nayak who wrote the foreword for this version of the masterpiece. My sincere thanks to Mr. Satya Patnaik and Mr. Ashok Parida at Black Eagle Books for publishing this book.

Dr. Tapan Kumar Panda

Pune
01-01-2023

CONTENTS

Five Ways to Kill Ramaa

Preface

Ramaa looked gorgeous, draped in a saree and adorned with jewels. But why would she listen to anyone? She wore stylish clothes and was a fashion victim. Her memory triggers my thoughts, and I envisage my pulling the trigger on her.

I still remember Ramaa draping herself in a saree for the first time. This happened on a hot and humid summer night. She was promoted to standard nine, and I was in the final year of my school life. The session was likely to begin after the summer vacation. In mid June in that humid weather, thenthree of us, I, Ramaa, and Ramaa's elder brother Tiku were sitting on the roof of a white building next to the wood yard in the center of the city. I was elated and expressed my gratitude towards God as, till then, Bikas was not in any way in Ramaa's life.

The single-storied white building belonged to Ramaa's uncle, the wood yard owner, and a plumbing contractor. He always paid the highest subscription, and his half-empty wood yard accommodated the theatre artists who were performing the play 'Subhadra Harana.'The house's rooftop was brimming with people who belonged to an affluent family and among them were 'we,' the trivial, rooted, soaked in sweat. I was more inclined towards movies rather than theatre, but Ramaa's eagerness to watch the play was triggered by temptation, and I accompanied them.

I have known Ramaa since her childhood as I frequently visited Tiku. She was a sloppy mess and had unkempt hair covered with dandruff, which is why her hair was shaved often. Her clean-shaven head made me visualize an ape. In the fourth standard, Ramaa came to school in her faded blue dress with a clean-shaven head. Subsequently, in the next two years, Ramaa's living room became a place to enact the play where Ramaa and I acted like a couple and Tiku as a tutor. Ramaa draped in Kuni aunty's saree, decked out in jewel and vermilion on her forehead - I fantasized about Ramaa in the same attire and beauty when I was thirteen.

The play began with a large crowd and the air intoxicated with radiance bewildered the spectators. The character of Arjuna was brilliantly enacted by a strong and stout man with lustful eyes. In contrast, Subhadra was played by Kuna, a third gender, because the previously chosen actress refused to act. Kuna was older than me, and his father was a daily labourer who fetched water from the hand pump and supplied it in the houses. I would like to narrate an incident related to Kuna. At the annual day celebration of the girl's school, entry of males was strictly prohibited. Kuna disguised himself in a *burkha* to evade the police but was caught red handed as the police could see his shoes which he could not hide underneath the *burkha*. He was beaten black and blue. This incident was highlighted in the newspaper the following day. The same chap who was thin as a kitten, tall like a bamboo tree, was dressed up to enact as Subhadra.

I could notice a sudden change in Ramaa's behavior. She became calm and conscious and hurried to go back home. I was taken aback. She insisted on taking a rickshaw and did not pay heed to my proposal of dropping her on my bicycle. We reached her house, and she knocked at the door. The jingle of the door chain corresponded with the interlude music played at the theatre. The next day Tiku again invited me to watch the play. I was not keen to watch it. I always agreed to accompany him because I longed for Ramaa's company. Tiku informed me that Ramaa wouldn't be able to join us as she had attained puberty the previous night and would abide by the customs of the society. I was ignorant regarding girls reaching puberty as there was no girl child in our family. In my ignorance, I asked Tiku, 'Is Ramaa suffering from fever?' Tiku answered that she was sitting alone in a room. I didn't pay much attention to what he said and moved out from there, riding my bicycle, and headed towards the same betel shop where I spent most of my youth although I was not addicted to betel.

After three days, there was a grand celebration in Ramaa's house, preceded by Satyanarayan Puja. Ladies of all age groups attended the function. I was awestruck when I saw Ramaa among the group of ladies because I saw her for the first time draped in a saree. She looked like a beautiful rose in her pink saree. She appeared grand. She looked like a bride, but I could never see her because, fifteen years after this incident, she eloped with Bikas and solemnized her marriage in court. I still sigh at the panoramic view, which is a never-ending thirst. I wonder! A saree can bring such a transformation in a girl!

Ramaa was giggling. Oh! She stopped as soon as she saw me. Her attitude towards me was never favourable, but her first saree-draped mature figure transfigured me into a grown man. It was a puzzle, hard to crack, a heart filled with despair!

BIKAS AND RAMAA

Bikas's personality enticed Ramaa. She could visualize the reflection of Saddam Hussein's personality in Bikas, which made her take an immoderate decision to elope with him and tie the knot. We realized that Saddam Hussein was a hero of the bygone days who was preceded by David Hadley, the most seductive personality of the present era. But, Ramaa paid no heed. As stated by Ramaa, Saddam Hussein had a towering figure, and a robust character that stood before her. I wonder! Why was Ramaa so much captivated by the look of Bikas Goel alias Bikas? He belonged to a typical Marwadi family, though relatively affluent but unappealing. Ramaa left no stone unturned to freak out on the good looks of Bikas. She was put under a spell by his charm . Oops! What an irony! Saddam Hussein versus Bikas! No ways! Oh! Bikas rode a bullet motorcycle, was a non-vegetarian, smoked and drank, and was bearded like a pard. Was that a reason enough to get infatuated? If so, why couldn't she marry Rajan Saklani, who bore a striking resemblance to V.S Naipaul? Ramaa justified her action and, of course, succeeded in marrying Bikas.

I was a scapegoat in this whole affair. Tiku, also Bikas's friend, could have helped them. But no. I suspect that Ramaa had decided to play a safe game, using me to accomplish her mission. Her dictatorship was quite evident. I became a witness in their marriage, and a photographer was hired to click the photos and shoot a video as proof of their marriage. After completing the marriage registration formalities, the duo went to a hotel to spend their time at leisure. We followed them sincerely as paid companions waiting eagerly to carry out the tasks assigned. Thud! The door was closed all of a sudden on our faces and was not opened even when the time for haiving meals arrived.

I could very well perceive that Bikas was like a fishbone stuck in my throat. I could neither gulp it nor spit it out. My bitterness for Bikas increased with time. I always tried to find a way out to ruin this prospering liaison. For the first time, I met Bikas on a football ground. He was the goalkeeper. He wasn't agile like a deer as he was a clumsy fellow. Though he boasted of being a good goalkeeper, he didn't prove to be... Alas! We lost the match. The way he went off riding his bullet motorcycle wearing a sports jersey after the game with Tiku as a pillion rider, gave us an inkling of what was going to happen? Ramaa was no more my treasure trove.

I concede Ramaa was never my gold mine. I could never digest that she could be an inexplicable passion and desire for someone. It was 'unrequited love.' Her dispassionate, inexpressive look was enough to suppress my feelings for her, which ultimately floated in the air like a water bubble. I was curious to know about her relationship with Bikas. I could feel the vibes. I could see the metamorphosis. 'Metamorphosis' of Ramaa from a caterpillar to a butterfly at the sight of Bikas.

I still remember Bikas in a shirt printed with a calendar motif. Maybe it was in vogue. Rich people have their way of dressing, so did Bikas. Ramaa's happiness knew no bounds as she invited me to have a look. I was awed! Ramaa was in her shorts and tops pulled at my heartstrings.

The city where Ramaa preferred to go for a court

marriage was a hub for people resorting to civil marriages. Las Vegas is the most talked about place in the world for prompt weddings and at swift divorces, and so was this city. I still wonder! Why did Ramaa pull me into this episode of her life when false witnesses for marriages were abundantly available? I sensed that Ramaa was more anxious than Bikas for this marriage. I still recollect those fond memories of the day on my way to the destination city for Ramaa's marriage. Her giggles still echo in my ears, her wavy open hair took me to the height of passion, and the fragrance of her body was ecstasy.

Many eligible couples on the bus were heading for their ultimate destination, but I think I was the only witness among all the witnesses who had a fake smile on their faces and a heart filled with venom. Maybe it was my enviousness. Bizarre brain work engulfed me. Still, my heart pounded for Ramaa.

WHY KILL RAMAA?

Ramaa always allured me with her winsomeness. Her laxity of morals and excessive liberty would result in a disaster. It might have instigated me to do the devilish act of slaying Ramaa. Why not? 'There was no limit to the moral baseness of the man of avarice.' It was more than flesh and blood could endure. It's true, she escaped, like the sand slipping through one's fingers. Ramaa had everything to make her contented and even happy. The intimacy and fulfilment of desire of Ramaa and Bikas cobbled together made me nutty. I envisioned killing Ramaa in my mind.

THE FIRST ATTEMPT

The first attempt was an opportunity rendered by Ramaa herself. I thought it was perfect to accomplish my task to slay Ramaa. Ramaa invited me to visit their store in the evening as there was a big surprise waiting for me. Her words pierced my heart. I had a sharp feeling of the butcher's knife tearing me into pieces. I switched on the radio, tuned to Bibidh Bharati, and listened to the old songs shamelessly to divert my mind. I was getting ready to proceed towards Marwadi Pada when suddenly there was a power cut, and I couldn't trim my beard.

The surprise that waited for me was not only for me but also for the whole city. Bikas had planned to revamp his cloth store by placing nine mannequins attired in sarees and salwar kamees; having firmly implanted them in a glass case gleaming in the open porch of the store.

This was an attempt made for the first time in the city to introduce a new concept of showcasing. Arrangements were made to serve mouth-watering snacks to the guests. The local MLA and press reporters were invited on this occasion. Most of the people present there were our friends and a few businessmen. As soon as I reached the place, I was greeted by Bikas with open arms and a loud scream. He said, 'Look! Here comes our broken-hearted man'. He came near me, pulled my cheeks, kept me on a tight rein, and introduced me to the people present over there. I was praised as Ramaa's friend and a silent philosopher. I could very well figure out the latent criticism. I was addressed as Udas Mohanty by Bikas. Perhaps it was just the sound of the word that had triggered the sudden annoyance. He could have addressed me as Devdas, but no. I felt as if I was lost in the ocean where my new introduction subdued my absolute identity.

The MLA was expected to arrive soon. In the meantime, the bare mannequins made up of gypsum or fiberglass and artificial hair on their head were carried from the rooftop to downstairs in the glass case. Suddenly Ramaa entered the room dressed in a glittering lehenga choli, and a white stole epitomizing the beauty of the tinsel town left the onlookers in awe. She came near me and dragged me towards the staircase. Bikas told me to go upstairs where a few of my friends enjoyed the evening.

I understood what he meant. It had happened many a times before that I had accompanied Bikas at the end of the day to relax with a bottle of beer. But I was surprised when Ramaa dragged me towards the basement instead of the rooftop. The dark narrow passage of the cellar and its stinking smell left me half unconscious. Ramaa came close to me and said, 'Listen! Don't say it to anyone; as soon as the MLA enters, you will switch off the main switch'. I was taken aback. 'Let it happen,' Ramaa said. She said she would enter the glass case, and the crowd that had gathered there would be mesmerized to see a live mannequin among the lifeless mannequins when the light was switched on. This will be a surprise for everyone present, including Bikas. I couldn't gather the courage to contradict Ramaa. She showed me the panel board fixed to the wall of the basement.

Before the MLA could be welcomed decently, darkness engulfed the room. People ran helter-skelter for an alternative arrangement to light up the area. The area was lit up in a few minutes. The atmosphere transposed into something commanding and beautiful. The luminous glass box placed with the mannequins looked like an abode of the deathless. In between the six white and three African mannequins, stood Ramaa with the same expression on her face, which could have easily eluded a beholder. The MLA inaugurated the mannequin display and keenly looked at the face of the first mannequin and was bewildered. Not only the MLA but Bikas and the crowd were also astounded. Ramaa broke her silence and waved at the press reporters and declared that she would place herself in the glass case until the store was closed and strike a pose like a mannequin.

Till late hours there was hustle and bustle in the store, especially in front of the mannequins. The MLA also left the place. But I wonder! whether the guests liked Ramaa's so-called dRamaatic act. But I couldn't notice a vision of gray eyes in Ramaa; it was obliterated. Slowly the crowd became thin, and I saw Bikas sitting at the store counter motionless and still. Ramaa paid no attention; she was engrossed in swanking. A lively wire comprised of anger and bitterness ran through my body. I thought it was time now to uproot this venomous entity. I didn't give it a second thought; I quickly went to the rooftop, fetched the kerosene bottle placed next to the lantern, and went straight to the basement.

I could see the bright glass case of the mannequin through the darkness of the basement. Silently, I spilled kerosene all over the floor and lit the fire. I left the place with the keys of the glass case in my pocket. In the meantime, I joined Bikas, and the glass case was engulfed with fire within no time. Some of them believed that this was one more trick played by Ramaa, which would be over in no time. But it wasn't so…Ramaa was crying out for help, fluttering like a blind owl, trying out ways to escape from the glass case. She was trying her best to control the fire and save her life. She might have seen me through the glass case, might have pleaded to open the door of the glass case, but I ignored it. Suddenly I saw Bikas trying to break the glass case forcefully, and I joined the race. Bikas lost his consciousness. I left the place stealthily before the arrival of the police, ambulance, and fire brigade.

While going through the newspaper the following morning, I came across the photos of the mannequins and the MLA along with whom Ramaa had posed for a photograph. There was nothing printed regarding the outbreak of fire in the store. I turned the pages of the newspaper, apprehending that it might have been published on some other page. My mother entered the room with the breakfast plate and asked me why I didn't have my food before sleeping last night? She also informed me that there was a call from Ramaa in the morning. I was surprised. My mother looked at my bare body and asked about the marks on it. I recollected the incident but wondered, could dreams be turned into reality?

THE SECOND ATTEMPT

It's (had been) almost two years now. My relationship with Ramaa was as good as dishwater. I still couldn't free myself from Ramaa's slavery; and what boldness was there for a scrub of a servant to speak before his master? I could notice that in the last few months, Ramaa had blossomed like a flower. She had a convincing charm that inspired others. She was similar to the Kalpavriksha, which possesses the quality of good wealth comparable to the sun having mass splendour on earth. I thought the basic logic behind her transformation was maybe her food habits, but a question lingered in my mind and baffled me. Was Ramaa pregnant? Was she carrying Bikas' child! This was an excellent reason enough to slay Ramaa.

Sunday was usually a day of rest for Bikas, but he spent half a day till noon to record his business and the bills. Ramaa also spent her day at leisure cooking delicious cuisine for Bikas and sometimes went to the beauty salon to enhance her beauty. Ramaa eagerly waited for the weekend as Bikas was engrossed in his business during weekdays. After Bikas came back at noon, the day was all theirs. Thus, the perfect time to visit Ramaa was after 10 am. Still, I wanted to cross-check Ramaa's availability.

Bikas said that Ramaa was available. He was bent over the papers in his office and wholly engrossed in his work. He was surprised to see me so early in the morning and asked me if I had any other intention for my visit in an accent of criticism. He instructed me to wait and have lunch together. I stood there for a while to hatch my plan before execution.

It was a double-storied building where the ground floor was occupied by Bikas's parents, and a staircase led to the first floor, which was occupied by the couple. It seemed Bikas had remodeled the house after his marriage according to Bombay's architectural pattern. As it was a Sunday, all the nearby shops in Marwadi pati were closed.

I swiftly climbed the staircase in nimble feet like a cat and rang the bell. No one saw me. I could hear Saibaba's bhajan being played on the ground floor, but why wasn't Ramaa opening the door even after ringing the bell so many times? Suddenly I could hear the footsteps behind the door. I immediately kept my fingers on the view glass. I could hear the giggles of Ramaa. She said,' I know you are Bikas. Are you trying to scare me? How come you finished your work so soon'? I was silent! Ramaa was a little annoyed and instructed me to wait there for some time as she was taking a bath. Suddenly she laughed and told me to come in.

She kept the door half open for a second, caught hold of my shirt, and pulled me inside the room. I was dumbfounded, too perplexed to beat soundly, and unable to speak. Ramaa stood there au naturel! I could see water dripping down her hair and foam over her body. I suddenly imagined a scene from a movie where a lady comes out of the bathroom in a robe but....

It took some time for Ramaa to understand the situation. She realized, screamed, and ran towards the bathroom; I followed her swiftly like a deer and entered the bathroom. Ramaa recognized me, fear unnerved her, and she trembled. She could not make out how to cover her bare body; she covered her bosom with her palm and stuck to the wall. The bathtub was half-filled with water, sunray penetrated through the stained glass window, and the same colored bulb glowed above the full-size mirror. I was standing so close to Ramaa that I could only see her face, but the mirror reflected the voluptuous image. Ramaa was quickly getting back to normalcy. I thought not to waste any more time and to execute my plan.

Ramaa was without a stitch. I have seen the picture of a nude woman only in books but not in reality. This account of Ramaa didn't thrill me. It was obnoxious. Ramaa had put on a little bit of weight. Out of curiosity, I asked Ramaa.' Are you pregnant'? She became aggressive and said,' Why are you so anxious? Why are you interested to know'? I screamed, 'You wretched woman'! I turned into a ferocious animal. I pounced on my prey, held her by the neck, and pressed her throat brutally. Ramaa was suffocated to death. I could see her defenceless body, eyes bulging out, a spate of blood trickling down her nose, and her diamond nose pin glittering in the light.

I planked down the lifeless body on the bathroom floor and turned off the water tap of the bathtub, which was packed to the brim to avoid the spilling of water on the floor. Then I cleaned everything around, which had my fingerprints with my handkerchief to exterminate all the evidence. I had a glance at Ramaa; for a second, I thought of wiping the blood on her cheeks, but the next moment I recollected the words written in a book 'A blood-stained piece of cloth is the greatest evidence to catch a culprit.'

I could accomplish my mission in an hour but felt a little sad for Bikas. What would happen when he returned at noon and knocked at the door? Who would be there to open the door? No one. I bolted the door from outside and stealthily climbed down the stairs. I felt like calling Bikas and informing him that I couldn't make it to meet Ramaa this Sunday, most probably would meet her the following Sunday.

The phone was ringing continuously, but Bikas didn't receive my call. I saw Bikas standing near me and saying.' I am sitting just a few feet away; why are you calling me over the phone, and what have you been thinking for the past one hour? I am done for the day. Let's go!'

THE THIRD ATTEMPT

Lord Sudarshana is worshipped along with the three deities, Lord Jagannath, Balabhadra, and Subhadra; similarly, the Bullet motorcycle of Bikas adored Ramaa's house. After marriage, Ramaa had gained control over it. The sideburns or opening the cork of the beer bottle to guzzle or the cigarette which kindled between the fingers of Bikas didn't captivate Ramaa. It was the bullet that symbolizes the vigor and vitality of Bikas. To plop down as a pillion rider decked out in jeans and sunglasses, inch closer to Bikas, meandering throughout the city always raised an eyebrow among the onlookers.

Bikas's reckless driving disseminates the crowd, terrorizing them. I once heard Ramaa saying how they went to the riverside on a full moon night, stretching their arms like the wings of a bird and posed like the Titanic hero Leonardo DiCaprio and the heroine Kate Winslet. The latter posed near the ship's mast just before the devastating episode. I murmured to myself and said; one day, the bullet will have the ill fate of the Titanic.

Time moved forward; the bullet never met with an accident, nor did the duo succumb to any fatal injuries. However, the road was always busy with lorries, buses, and sometimes with sixteen-wheeled carriers. Still, whenever I went out on my bicycle, my mother would always have apprehensions in her mind. She would pray to God for my well-being and safe homecoming.

One day in the afternoon, I was reading a 'Monthly detective' story when I noticed a fat white cat, as white as snow sitting on the boundary wall and looking straight at me through the window. I dislike cats. A terrible idea fastened my thought as this white cat was causing inconvenience in the house by feasting on fish and milk. There was a small ornamental mirror on my table, which my mother had brought along with her during her marriage. Sometimes I looked at the mirror in a state of despair, occasionally checking my appearance and sometimes mocking myself. A ray of bright sunlight descended upon my bed; I quietly took the mirror and showed it in the sunlight. The mirror reflected the sunny rays and dispersed it profoundly. I turned the direction of the mirror towards the open window where the white cat gave her feet a rest, and the intense reflection from the mirror blinded the cat, and she fell with a thud.

I could trace the ice-clad mountain, but there was no trace of a sea to give an appearance of solidity to Titanic. I inspected the prime roads of the city and places to teem with effective execution of the plot. I always carried my mother's hand mirror along with me. Finally, I could get a suitable location,' A Public Library.' There was a small park behind it and the first air-conditioned film hall of the city on the other side park. The town's busiest road goes through the film hall and bifurcates in front of the library, leading the left side road towards the bus stand and city hospital and the right side road leading to the film hall and further towards the railway station.

The library building was three-storied. The ground floor had a City bank ATM on the left side; the rest of the space was partially occupied by the Census office, and the rest was a reading room for the general public. The first and second floors had a vast collection of books that only a library member could enjoy. They also had a balcony on each floor facing west, receiving abundant sunlight and warmth. The terraces were covered with wooden and glass panels to prevent the scorching heat. I entered the library impersonating as a person enquiring about the membership. I could discern that the balcony on the library's first floor was the most appropriate place to execute my plan. The road was clearly visible through the square-shaped glass with wooden and glass panels, and the sun rays penetrated through the glass and reflected on the wall creating a crossword puzzle. This place wasn't frequented by many.

I placed myself near the balcony railing as if I was looking at the road and quickly positioned the mirror in my hand on the glass. The mirror reflected the rays, and the reflection appeared like a blotting paper on the road. Now it was time to test. An old man was on his way in a bicycle laden with bags, and the reflection of the mirror blindfolded him. He applied a sudden brake, stopped, and looked here and there. He got down from the bicycle, walked for a while, and rode his bike. After a time, a police jeep was on its way when the rays from the mirror reflected on the windshield and blindfolded the driver. The jeep screeched! And halted. I could understand that my idea had worked. I left the library in a very casual way whistling a cinema song and crossed the parked police jeep.

It was a Sunday. I worked in a LIC office, and in a true sense, everyday was like a holiday for me as people seldom visited this office. But the Public Library was closed on Sunday; how would I have executed my plan? Even if I had invited Ramaa and Bikas to come to the library, they would not show interest, so the best thing was to ask them for the matinee show of a film.

I went through the last page of the newspaper and found out that the old film of the actor Raj Kumar was on the reel in matinee shows for the past one week in the air-conditioned cinema hall. That day the film Heer Ranjha of Rajkumar was on the revolution. Ramaa likes the actor Raj Kumar.' Mother India was broadcasted on TV, and a scene that portrayed Raj Kumar, a man with an amputated hand smoking bidi, enthralled Ramaa. She read somewhere that

Raj Kumar used wigs to cover his head. However, even the renowned stars of the era couldn't stand firm as co-stars opposite him. According to Ramaa, even Amitabh Bachchan also dithered to act with Raj Kumar; therefore, the couple accepted the Heer Ranjha matinee show invitation.

I started from home at 2 pm. I had the mirror in my pocket, which personified the large iceberg which was the cause of the wreck of the titanic. It was a Sunday afternoon, and the security guard was still on his duty, half drowsy, near the library. I looked here, and hem and haw entered the ATM though I didn't have a card. I fiddled with the board of the ATM machine, quietly climbed the stairs, and went to the top floor. The library was locked, and the balcony was empty. I chose a square glass from the balcony panel where my hands could reach and break the glass, but the shattering sound of the glass couldn't get anyone's ear because of the noisy road.

It was almost 2.45 pm. The sun was shining brightly, and I could see the couple in their bullet speeding from the west like a ship drifting forward, breaking the waves. The roaring sound of the engine was resounding in my heart. Ramaa was sitting at the back very closely to Bikas, placing her hands on Bikas's hand as if she was navigating the ship as a co-captain. Luckily Bikas wasn't using the sunglasses. I was alert as if I had been keenly waiting for this moment for a long time. As they came closer, the mirror in my hand sparkled like phosphorous before Bikas could take a turn. Bikas wiped his eyes, and before he could gain control over himself, he was blindfolded by the reflection of the mirror, and the motorcycle skidded. Ramaa fell like a broken wing of an airplane. Bikas couldn't realize the situation immediately, and they were seized by a speeding Innova.

This was the end of 'Titanic.' The sun wasn't shining brightly; it was twilight. I couldn't see my reflection in the mirror, and I was mocking myself in that dimness. At that moment, I received a phone call from Bikas. He was angry and coaxed me to send them to watch the Heer Ranjha. He said, 'Is Raj Kumar suitable to play the role of Romeo at that this age'? He said that he didn't enjoy the show as the actor played flute under the tree most of the time and it was a black and white film, although Ramaa enjoyed it. He asked why didn't I join them for the film. Ramaa was eagerly waiting for me.

I disconnected the phone without uttering a single word. What would I have said? A state of gloominess enveloped the whole atmosphere. I switched on the bedside lamp, and a dull blue light reflected on my face. I felt sick as a dog. I showed the mirror in the splash of blue light, which created an arch on the roof though insensate.

THE FOURTH ATTEMPT

The train sped on. I was busy observing the grey smoke trail coming out from the chimney of the factories, one or two railway crossing, people waiting there, one or two narrow streams of the river, and a bridge over it. On the train, I crossed the green fields and the horizon of themountains. The train was covering the distance running between between Jamshedpur-Chibasa and Chakradharapur.

It was not a general compartment but a luxurious railway salon meant for officers on inspection duty. We (I, Ramaa, and Bikas) were consuming beer, along with the high profile railway officer Mr .T.Rajeswar, the head of Chakradharpur Railway division. We played cards and had roasted chicken and whiskey at night in the railway salon. He had invited Ramaa and Bikas to celebrate his anniversary with much fun and frolic in the railway siding.

None of us had experienced the comforts of a railway salon before. I didn't have the privilege to travel by AC first class in my life. While in college, I appreciated the travelers traveling in the Madras Mail AC compartment, although I never got a chance to enter the compartment. Once Gouri and I traveled by Jagannath Express to Kolkata without a ticket sitting in the RMS compartment, along with Goloka, who worked in RMS. Near Balasore, the higher officer came for inspection, and we tried to hide among the RMS staff. We started stamping the letters and putting them in the bags allotted for Balasore irrespective of their exact destination.

Today, I was there, enjoying drinks and playing cards in this luxurious railway salon. It was a sunny afternoon, the month of June, and two waiters wearing gloves in their hands were ready to serve us tea, but we preferred to have a beer. It was an air-conditioned salon, but Bikas had opened the buttons of his white shirt, and I could see Ramaa was in her blue faded shorts. I can never forget the way she adorned her pelvis with a thick silver chain. Mr. T.Rajeswar's wife was in Rajahmundry, and he was flirting with Ramaa in this railway salon. Bikas should have been be ashamed of masculinity.

Once again, my heart became venomous. I left the drawing-room of the exquisite salon decorated with glass panels, pendant lights, and antique furniture and went to the corridor. It was almost dark outside, and I could see birds flying back to their nests. I walked through the hall towards the end of the salon. There were two rooms adjacent to the sitting room. Maybe one was occupied by the high-ranked official and the other one by Ramaa and Bikas. Perhaps I would get a place in the guard's room to sleep, but who knows whether it will be possible to rest or not as it was a celebration night, I thought.

I walked back through the corridor and went towards the engine. I could hear their shrill voice and crackle. Maybe they didn't miss me in their drunken state. I never knew that a railway salon is the only compartment attached to a unique engine. I entered the engine room, which was murky and looked for the driver. Varghese was a dark, tall, thin man in his uniform and was looking out through the windshield into the open sky. He staggered and wished me again. When I met him on the platform for the first time, I noticed that he had very expressive eyes, which reflected agony. I offered him a cigarette which he was reluctant to take but later on accepted. It was a diesel engine, so there was no smoke or fire, but the place was gloomy. The headlight of the train was flashing.

I spent a lot of time with Varghese. There was no one in the lobby when I returned. Maybe they went to their rooms to refresh themselves before dinner. I usually wear the same clothes from the morning till evening, so it wasn't a hassle for me. I went down the corridor again, opened the compartment's door, and stood awhile. It was almost 9 pm, but still, it was warm outside. It was pitch dark on both sides except for the bright headlight of the train. A shooting star fell from the sky, analogous to Ramaa creeping into my life.

By the time I returned to the lobby, the atmosphere was revamped. The sofa cover was changed, the chandelier was gleaming, on one side was a bar made up of mahogany wood on which whiskey soda was kept and on the other side was a table covered with a check red table cloth on which plates, knives, and forks were arranged along with four candle stands. A perfect arrangement for a candlelight dinner! A melodious old cinema song was being played on a piano that could be heard through the inbuilt speaker; in the pantry, a sumptuous dinner was cooked, and the aroma filled the place.

I was standing in the lobby and appreciating the squared planning of Mr. T.Rajeswar. In the meantime, Ramaa entered with a burst of piercing laughter. She looked at me and asked, 'Where did you go in-between'? Didn't you like it? I shook my head and left it to her to infer its meaning. Ramaa was wearing a long white gown that projected her dark soul, bare feet, loose hair, eyes pancaked with kajal, and a hand wearing a dozen silver bangles. Ramaa is like Tanaz's choreographer. Whatever she does is a style.

Whatever I had suspected happened! Ramaa didn't drink, Rajeswar sir drank consciously, but Bikas got drunk and lost his senses. Almost no one had the dinner properly, the lights of the chandelier were switched off, candles were extinguished, and the magic began. Ramaa and T.Rajeswar clapped and danced. The waiters left, and I was the only one standing near the bar with a whiskey glass in hand and was watching this episode. Ramaa didn't know how to dance. She was just hoping like a crow and moving from here and there and Rajeswar sir to taught her ballet to hold her hand and her waist. I couldn't tolerate it anymore and left the place.

The corridor was dark. The wind speed was less, and there was no trace of human habitant outside. It was dark , surrounded by forest. I could see the forest fire at a distance, which looked like a yellow garland in this darkness.

I lit a cigarette to ease myself and walked towards the engine room. I still could hear western music playing in the lobby. I doubted whether Ramaa would protect herself from Rajeswar that night.

Varghese looked at me and was frightened as if he had seen a ghost. Of course, there was no reason for me to go to the engine room so late at the night, but I never expected that his large expressive eyes filled with agony would look terrorized. He was fumbling; he held my hand and asked why I had come there so late at night?

He said, 'if you have come, then don't go back. Take this way and get down.' He held my hand and took me near the door.

I became suspicious.' Was he going to throw me out of the speeding train'?

After that, many things happened at a time. Varghese did something, and the train stopped in the mid of a bridge, and the engine's headlight went off. 'Come, come, come quickly', he said and dragged me out of the train. We crossed the bridge in a few seconds, and in that darkness, he made me run into the paddy field. From a distance, I could see the candles lit in the salon lobby, which was dim, but the music was much louder. Maybe Ramaa and Rajeswar were doing Salsa.

After some time, an unbelievable thing happened. I could see an orange light under the bridge, and there was an explosion within a second. In that explosion, the bridge collapsed, the engine and the compartment broke into pieces and flew in the air. Before I could realize anything, Varghese held me tight and lowered my head. Maybe some debris flew over our heads. When everything became silent, I stood up and saw that everything had turned into a heap of garbage; I couldn't even find Varghese lying next to me. I always looked for a plan to kill Ramaa, but I never knew that her fate had stored such a terrible death for her. Good Bye! Dear emotional blackmailer, did you achieve anything flirting with the south Indian guy towards the end of your life?

The next day I was asleep till 9 am, and a phone call from Bikas woke me up. He told me that we are supposed to go to Jamshedpur as the Regional Manager has invited us to have a beer together in the railway salon.

' Yes,' I replied. I will be there in an hour.'

'No,' he said. The program was cancelled as the Maoists blew up the bridge near Chaibasa. 'It will take some time to normalize the situation.'

THE FIFTH ATTEMPT

I saw Ramaa in my dream. She was in a black saree with a zari border. She was standing in her maternal house courtyard where her first saree draping ceremony had been organized, and for the first time, I had felt like marrying her. There was no one else in the yard except Ramaa and me. I made up my mind to tell her everything . The consequences hardly mattered).

I: Look! Ramaa, until you are dead, I can't have you. Until you die, your eyes will be roving around. I am exhausted now with my plans to kill you. Why are you not dying?

Ramaa: (Laughs)-'My dear mournful sweetheart, how do I know what's on your mind? Do you know where my life is? Pampering me a bit, look into my eyes and just say once that you love me. I will hear these words and die.'

The Mirror

I was staying in Cuttack. At that time, I was young and a student of Ravenshaw College. I had used 'Hairless Feet' (*Viloma Paada*) in one of my poems. It was an important idiom used to describe protagonist's sexual urge. The sensual aspect has an increase or decrease as per the presence of hair in different parts of the body. For a few days, it was a subject of debate and discussion among us. No one knew that Chhabi's yellow double storied house's staircase landing at Chandni Chowk was the place where 'Hairless Feet' (*Viloma Paada*) was conceived for the first time.

The landing was spacious and in the middle of a smooth and red cemented staircase. It was so spacious that even if two of them were standing and talking, the third could easily walk thrpugh. A big full-size mirror was in the landing area in which one can see an image from top to bottom and can estimate about one's movement up or down on the stairs.

Chhabi was a girl from a joint family. There exists many restrictions in a joint family, including falling in love. She had her siblings and cousins who crowded the house. So I could only get a chance to be close to her at the landing of the staircase. The mirror always warned us about the intruder into our privacy. Once after watching the '*Pakiza*' film, when I was kneeling and kissing the feet of Chhabi, who wore a mini skirt, I saw her smooth, hairless legs. In the meantime, I had already started shaving my beard, and Chhabi has started going to the parlour for body waxing.

It was almost fifty years back. I have been staying in a foreign land for forty years. Today in Prafulla Mohanty (the famous Odia artist and painter) 's London home at Sussex Street, while climbing the staircase, I saw a huge mirror framed in Rosewood placed exactly in the landing area very similar to the mirror in Chhabi's house. On that day, he went down the staircase in a hurry. I couldn't realize at what time he alighted from the upper floor. He was a young man with spectacles. His image reflected on my eyes for a second while he went downstairs. I thought, whom did I see at that moment, was it a reflection on the mirror, or did he really came down, as if the mirror was a passage to walk up and down.

Prafulla Mohanty and his British friend Derek Moor weren't there at home. During summer, in August, hardly anyone stays at home in London. When I was studying at Kernel University, the United States of America, I had met Prafulla Mohanty. Whenever I travel from the USA to India or Europe in between, I stay at Prafulla Mohanty's house in London. He and Derek liked me a lot, and his house was always crowded as if it's a zoo. People from Odisha and even other states and countries were his guests. Maybe the young man who went down quickly was one of his guests.

The young man vanished before I could turn my face to look at him. I went upstairs and looked outside through the large window in my room towards the street. It was almost 10 o'clock. The chemist and grocery shops were already open. But in front of his house was the 'Queen of

Hearts' shop which had not been opened as it was open till late last night. The house was in the West End, a very posh locality. It was constructed during the Second World War in the Georgian style. It had four to five floors, including the basement. Whoever stays in that house, Mr. Prafulla gives him a duplicate key of the front door. The young man who seemed as if he had come out from the mirror looked familiar, but I couldn't recognize him. He must have had a duplicate key of the house.

Few people were invited for lunch. Mr. Prafulla Mohanty and Derek were expected to arrive soon. Mr. Prafulla, an artist is a good cook, so there was a reflection of art in his cooking. All the colours in the food remained intact. To spend my time, I went to the basement studio of Mr. Prafulla. It was a big walk-in studio where sun rays filled the room. I found some of his paintings. A few of them were complete, and another set of incomplete lot. Paint tubes and brushes were lying here and there.

The layout of the basement was very unique. It was made up of different architectural styles. In the beginning, there was a fancy salon made in Baroque style: the wall, window, and furniture imitated theatrics. But one-fourth of the room was renovated in a modern style that was square and circular in shape. Mr. Prafulla works in this place, and his friends come here to have a drink with him. I sat where the sunrays were falling. I looked at the basement part designed in West Minister style, or the architecture was of Louis Fourteenth reign. The young man who seemed to come out from the mirror was sitting in a dark corner near the cupboard filled with books. He was wearing a spectacle and had a book in his hand. Uptill the roof, there was a narrow window which was covered with a thick silk curtain, and a ray of light passed through the curtain's narrow opening; he was engrossed reading a book in that light. He ignored the existence of another person in the house. His focus with the book made me think that it wasn't him, but I, who was sitting there.

Whenever I see books, I get captivated by their charm. In the basement, at the backside wall, there was an ample walnut-coloured book cupboard and I was feeling guilty for not noticing it earlier. I strolled towards the other end of the room, and I felt as if it took me ages to cover that distance. The young man looked at me and smiled when I reached the shelf. I could recognize him but wasn't very clear ON his identity. He had a brown moustache, dark eyes, and well-shaped lips.

'Hello! Are you from Odisha?' He smiled, and that indicated that he indeed was.

Anxiously I asked, 'From which place in Odisha'?

He said,' Cuttack .' I didn't know any other place in Odisha other than Cuttack. Was it adequate or inadequate? I couldn't guess.

'I also belong to Cuttack. Where do you stay in Cuttack?'

'Alamchand Bazaar, right in front of the Goswami Press.' I (then) asked him, 'What does your father do'?

He said that his father was a writer. There was a turmoil inside me. There was a sign of apprehension on his face. I looked at him and said, 'So, you are Devdas Chottaray?'

The smile on his face faded.

'You may be surprised, but my name is also Devdas Chottaray. The house about which you are talking also belongs to me. The incredible thing is that we both are meeting for the first time here in London, that too in 2011'.

He closed the book, glanced at me and said, 'No. It is 1964. I have never seen London as I stay in Cuttack and the summer vacation is in June. I am in the reading room of Kanika library reading a book.'

'Dostoyevsky'? I asked.

-Crime and Punishment, he said in a little uneasy manner, 'Has Raskolnikov already met Dounia?'

With a grin, he said, 'Not yet, I have just begun with the first few pages. Raskolnikov is suffering from fever. He is wearing an overcoat, standing on a bridge, and looking at the river in the afternoon.'

Though I knew, I didn't tell him that Raskolnikov's addiction won't leave him for life. . I only told him that I had read 'Crime and Punishment' thrice. It had always brought a change in my life whenever I read it.. I don't dare to reread it. It had brought in a cruel turn of my fate with every reading. I didn't dare read it again.

He stood up with the book. He was almost my height. He was wearing the same type of thick glass spectacle like me. He said,' I agree that there is some similarity between us. But you are older than me, yet you know very well how to weave your words into woofs.'

When I heard that I was older, unknowingly, my hands touched the scanty hair on my head .

'Why this question of enchantment? It is only my memory power. You can test me. In the drawing-room, where my father does his writing, there is a bookshelf with collected works of Shakespeare; My father scoled my sister who wrote her name in Odia and spilled ink on the first page of the book. There is a 1955 wooden cabinet model of HMV radio in our bedroom. Doesn't the magic eye of the radio glow like a cat's eye in the night? In a glass cupboard in the prayer rom, lies a silver medal, my father received when his play 'Other's Pen'(*Para Kalam*) was staged in Delhi. In the last room close to the chest, within the cloth rack is hanging my grandfather's walking stick which lay concealed in a four and a half feet rusted iron dagger. It has a blood bathed historical importance .'

I thought he must have accepted my argument and justification, but he said,' Wonderful! Few people also daydream; it's proved now. Who knows, maybe I am a dream, and you have conceived it in your mind'. I replied,' This argument also stands for you. Who knows, maybe you are the reality, and I am your dream'. He couldn't deny my justification.

Mr.Prafulla and Derek still hadn't returned. The guests also hadn't arrived for lunch. There was bright sunshine outside. I suggested for a walk outside. He agreed. When we came out of the basement and stood in the bright sunlight, I noticed that he was wearing a long, white sleeved shirt, with folded cuff, and a black cord trouser similar to the character of a poem in my English poetry book where Casabianca was standing alone on the board of the ship caught in fire. I also liked this combination. The Thames River was just a few minutes walk from Mr. Prafulla's house. We walked towards Battersea Park.

While walking on the Albert Bridge, I said, 'My past is your future. Do you want to listen?'

I didn't wait for his reply and said, 'Mother passed away long back, and my father expired just recently. He lost his power to recall. He looked at my mother's photograph and lived for twenty-five years, but, in the end, he couldn't recollect her name. He could only recognize me. Theaters are closed in Cuttack for a long time. Cuttack radio station was my father's fort, and now because of the television channel and FM radio, no one is interested in listening to it. My father didn't get any more chances to write a play for the theatre, and finally, he started writing stories for magazines. I have heard that *Mahanadi* and *Kathjodi* river water have moved away from their banks, and Balijatra is now being held in the sandy banks of the *Mahanadi*. Keshu's children have closed the betel shop and got a license to sell baby food. I have also heard that Ravenshaw college is now a university. I haven't been to Cuttack for a long time. After Akshaya Mohanty's death, there is no point in visiting Cuttack. My younger sister spoiled the first page of Shakespeare's collective work by spilling ink over it. Her granddaughter was born in America. Her name is Ariana.'

Without a glance at me, he gave the statement in a passive and soft voice. 'I can't understand what you are saying. Everything is okay at our house in Cuttack. There are two plays by my father that are being performed in the theatre though my mother still doesn't go to watch them. There is sarcasm towards communists in the play, but I like communism. I just finished reading the *'Communist Manifesto'*. Marx's arguments are incomparable. There is so much bewilderment, inequity, struggle, and confusion in this world that makes me restless.'

I had asked my father,'Why there is so much restlessness when I wake up? He said,'You are grown up now. Akshaya Mohanty is currently composing a new chorus, 'Youth.' I am writing the script. Cuttack is as it is. I don't know which river bank you are at, but I am walking along the riverside of *Kathjodi*. A river looks beautiful when the other side of the bank is visible. Look at my watch; it's now five-thirty, and the evening on the riverside is so calm!'.

In a few places, the river Thames is narrower than *Kathjodi*. One could see the other side. As per Big Ben, here it is noon time. It is lunchtime, and we have to go back home. Fifty years is a long time. Perhaps we are the same person, probably twins. But in these fifty years, the link connecting us was lost. I looked at the watch in his hand and realized that it was one of the first HMT watches made in India. My father paid ninety rupees through money order and had ordered this watch when I was doing my B.A. I didn't tell him that after a few years,This very watch would-be stolen in one of the hotels in Delhi. I didn't ask him, for whom did he write the song '*Eka ange atae rupa* (So much of beauty in one body)'? For whom did he walk in the college's empty corridors during summer vacation; for whom did he search for around the Sun-dial, for whom did he search for among the books in *Kanika* library. I knew that very soon, his dreams would be shattered. I observed him fondly.

We crept for some time. He was near me, but sometimes he became invisible momentarily like in a James Bond movie; 007 driven Aston Martin car vanishes like a silver ghost from the enemies' eye. While coming back, he spoke about his write-ups. He said, 'I have written maximum number of poems this year, almost every day. I can publish a book out of it'.

I could understand his excitement. I remembered Pablo Neruda. He had now reached that age when poetry came by itself into poet's imagination. When the heart is filled with remorse, poetry creeps in. I asked him, 'What will be the name of the book if you publish it?'

He immediately said, 'Nila Saraswati'.

I had this name in my mind for a long time though I didn't know the exact meaning. I couldn't tell him that it would take many more years to publish this book. He would be so engrossed in vested relationships and callous attitude that even if he tried to find himself among these, it would be difficult for him to find himself. The cover page would be a blue arch painted by Mr. Prafulla Mohanty. Now he asked me about my write-ups. I was unable to make him understand that when you try to write poetry at a certain age, it doesn't come into your imagination. Whatever I want to write or had written was just a repeatation.

I am he who knows his self-esteem,

not a little less,

its image in the mirror

in the glass and among the silence;

searching for others impression.

I am he, Oh! My silent friends,

who doesn't know, violence or pardoning,

None is powerful

than to forget;

If God has given

all the hatred of humanity,

despite my surprise

I am he, who is unabashed.

Over time, alone, different

broken and wonderful, for others

I am nothing,

I have never risen

the sword in any war,

I am an echo

empty and artificial...

Surprisingly, he looked at me, and asked, 'Did you write this?'

There was respect in his eyes.

-No, I only did the translation.

He asked excitedly, 'Whose poetry is this?'.

-'Jorgie Lui Borges.'

'Oh! Yes,'he jumped in excitement. 'I thought it was his poetry. I am a fan of Borges. I like his prose, poetry, and essay. He was a brilliant writer. He became blind towards the end of his life, wasn't he?'

'Yes, like Milton.' I said. Borges lost his eyesight gradually, like how the evening approaches slowly.

For rest of the time, both of us were silent again.

Finally, the poems of a poet brought us together.

When we entered the house, we could hear a lot of noise from the basement. I think lunch had begun. I said, 'Let's go to the room and freshen up.' Both of us climbed up the staircase together, and as per my habit, I looked at myself in the mirror, but I couldn't see my image. I could see the posterior of a young man entering the mirror swiftly dressed as Casabianca with a folded shirt sleeves near the elbow and black trousers. He seemed like a ship on fire in the blazing sunlight of the noon.

While Waiting for the Coffee

1. HAPPINESS AND SADNESS

'I haven't undergone such grief that will give you pleasure. I am fine! Im sorry that im fine)!' Bikas told Ramaa very sarcastically. It was for the second time that they were meeting after their separation. For the first time, they met at Santa Cruz airport. Almost five years back, Bikas went somewhere; he doesn't remember where. There was no way for him to collect information regarding Ramaa. They met by chance for a second time in the airport while hastily collecting their luggage in the trolley from different directions. They were lost in the whispers, the sound of the plane and the bright light of the airport. Both of them weren't prepared for this accidental meeting. They were like two birds crossing each other in a thunder and lightning; then suddenly came in front of each other and recognized in a second. They paused momentarily, turned back, and felt ashamed of having been caught, but they couldn't muster the courage to return or look back again. While walking forth, what did Bikas think? I don't know, but he grinded his teeth and said,'Bloody bitch!'

Today they met for the second time after a gap of five years. Nowadays, Bikas works in central school, and Ramaa had come to take someone's Ph.D. viva.

Both Bikas and Ramaa knew that there was indeed a chance of meeting each other. Maybe because of that, mentally they were well prepared. By mistake, when they met near the coffee counter after the examination, Ramaa asked Bikas, 'How are you'?

Bikas replied, 'I haven't passed through any grief, which can be a reason for your happiness. I am sorry!'

Ramaa didn't wait for her conscience to prick her for Bikas' self-satisfaction, and she uttered, 'Bloody bastard'!

2. LIE, SUSPICION, AND HELPLESSNESS

For the past one and half years, I had suspicion that Rekha was in love with Abid and trying to hide it from me. Last Sunday afternoon, evading everybody's eyes, when she returned to the lonely small house on the top floor to meet me, and post a rain shower, we tried to give warmth to each other in that December afternoon. But we couldn't. To test her, I asked

- Do you love Abid?

-Don't be silly

-Trying to fool me?

She screamed in protest as if she would pull down the roof.

-If you don't love him, say, 'Abid is a dog'!

She looked at me in astonishment.

-You don't love him, so say, 'Abid is a dog'. I forced her to say, and she uttered the word feebly in hesitation.

- No shout, bloody black dog.

- Bloody black dog.

Though Abid didn't have a dark complexion, he was dusky.

Her face turned pale; I thought of smoking but she couldn't tolerate the smell of cigarettes, so I pulled Rekha towards myself. It was raining intermittently and cold outside. There was no excitement or warmth in Rekha's acquiescence. Though it was unnatural, still, I consoled myself- No, she doesn't have any relationship with Abid, which she should respect.

-Bloody black dog!

I felt a little guilty. I remembered my insistence, but just after three days, on December 31st, Rekha eloped with Abid without my knowledge into the darkest corner of the bright new year.

What will I do?

Reenvision

Cring….cring…

The telephone rang. He lifted the phone. Before picking up, he thought for a while whether to extinguish the cigarette or not, but instead of doing so, he held it on his left hand. The telephone was on the right-hand side of the desk. Emerging smoke from the burnt cigarette on the left hand appeared like a whirlpool that spread slowly around the room.

As the room's windows were closed, movement of the smoke prolonged. There was a window air conditioner installed in the room, making it very cold although it was scorching heat outside in the June month.

-Hello!

-Hello!

-Who?

-Sir, I am Bata

- Who?

- I am Bata, the head assistant.

-Oh! What happened?

- Sir, he wants to be relieved from his duties today.

- Who is saying what?

-Sir, Goura… Gourang Majhi, the accountant. He is

stubborn and wants to get relieved today. I have already told you that he has been transferred to Sambalpur…

Bata disconnected the phone. He wanted to say 'wrong number', but forgot at that moment. Sometimes he thinks that he has conveyed the message, but most of the time, he has not.

The cigarette was almost half charred, but as the room was not airy, the dust was still intact on the cigarette. The room was new and well maintained; had an attached washroom, the windows were designed in a later stage as per the modern architecture. In the secretariat building, the interior facing windows were uniform. The parallel corners of the thirteen-storied, tall building reflected the sun-rays, that ttook the shape of a cubicular art screen. His old office was in the ancient city of another state, that stood testimony of British colonial architecture.

-Cring…Cring, again the telephone rang

-Hello!

-Hello! Sir

-Who?

- I am Bata, the head assistant.

The telephone got disconnected. The man called again…

- I think it's the wrong number; he told this time

- No, Sir, this is the correct number. I think you aren't able to recognize my voice. Since yesterday I have been suffering from a cough, cold, and throat infection. Sir, if you say I will immediately start working on the file…

- Which file? (He spoke as per his habit)

-Goura's relieving file, Sir, he wants to be relieved today; otherwise, he will be in a problem. Sir, kindly….

- What will I do? (He said in a feeble voice while disconnecting the phone)

He (had) joined here just five days back. Working days are from Monday till Friday, followed by two days of holidays, but it's not sufficient for him to go to Delhi and visit his family. He stays here in the Circuit House, and no one knows to him in this place. He doesn't have books, CDs and DVDs to spend time, the only way to spend time is to read the newspaper and watch television in the evening. They have taken away everything while he was vacating his old office; now his life is only limited to the empty office room and the circuit house. It's boring. He thought about how to spend the entire week.

-Cring... Cring... Again the telephone rang (This time cigarette wasn't in his hand)

-Hello!

- Will you come, sir? Again the same person.

He disconnected the phone, but it rang again.

-The telephone is getting disconnected again and again.

-- Abysmal service!

He thought he would say it's the wrong number, and in no way he is related to the telephone in the room, and he also doesn't know the telephone number. He wanted to say that he wasn't the person to whom the caller wanted to speak; at that moment, a bus went on the main road blowing the horn aloud. He couldn't understand how he could hear the loud sound in that closed room. He thought maybe it was because of the doppler effect. Many years back, he was a student of physics.

He was holding the telephone receiver but couldn't

say what he wanted to convey, and said, 'Tell me what else you want to say?

-What else will I say, sir? It's about Goura…

- About what? Who is Goura?

He became a little curious now. The feeling was of a slight shiver that ran down the spine when you touch the warm water.

-That Goura, sir, who kept his hand on your table and leaned forward, and you said,' Hands up.'

- On my table… There was no artificiality in his voice.

- Sir, did you forget. Just two months back. I…

Two months, even two weeks back, he wasn't there in this state.

-I was with you…

No, he didn't disconnect. It got disconnected. He was trying to understand the matter, and the telephone rang again.

-Cring… Cring...

-What happened then?

- What happened, with whom were you speaking?

A cheerful laugh of a lady was heard.

Oh! Swati, his wife, had called from Delhi. He became a little attentive. Swati spoke to him for five minutes and asked whether he ate lunch, when is he planning to come home, and then disconnected the telephone. It was chilly; a remnant of loneliness; a pain without agony.

He looked outside; it was blazing sun, and room inside, it was fantastic, and there was a window curtain covering the window glass. Between the mirror and the curtain, he could see a housefly moving around. He was restless. Twiddle thumbs. No work, no visitors, no invitations in the evening. In this hot and humid city, even cigarettes couldn't spark his interest. He suddenly remembered about a cigarette.

While smoking, he thought about the communication that happened over the phone, the birth of a story that also got muddled.

-Cring .. Cring…

- Hello! He said consciously

-Sir, It got disconnected again. I have been trying since then…

- He kept on saying something

- okay okay, tell

Though he wasn't smoking, he was now ready for the story.

-Do you remember Goura, whom I brought along with me? Gourang Majhi, the hefty man who was so nervous that he couldn't stand upright and leaned on your table. Slimy creature! When you said, 'Hands up', his breath stopped. His sister-in-law spoke, and he escaped from the situation…

-Sister in law?

Suddenly he became vocal

- Sir, sister in law. She is the reason behind this whole affair. That tall dusky, sharp-tongued girl in a *Kota Doria* saree was hiding behind Goura. When she saw her brother-in-law was nervous, she immediately came to the front and said, Excuse me, Sir…

The head assistant narrated everything so distinctly

and colorfully that he felt he had seen Goura and his sister-in-law. There was a cigarette in one hand and the telephone in the other hand. He kept his eyes closed and imagined Goura's sister-in-law. Her dusky color, sharp features, bright eyes, loose hair, and a mole on the upper lip. misfortune! Swati doesn't have a single mole on her porcelain body.

- What did her sister-in-law say? She was now part of the story.

- Sir, what didn't she say? Sir, you must have remembered, that girl constantly spoke for seventeen minutes at a stretch. You were looking at her, and then you permitted Goura's transfer.

- Oh! Tell me, what did she say? Goura's sister in law…

- Sir, she said everything frankly to you. She is almost half of the age of Goura. Her elder sister suffered from a stroke and is completely bedridden. She took care of both the children, and for the past ten years, she has been staying with Goura, and all her talents will go in vain if Goura isn't transferred to Sambalpur.

- Talent? He again tried to understand.

- Yes, Sir. The big-eyed sister-in-law of Goura is a star. She is well known in western Odisha. No one can sing the song *Rangabati, Rangabati* like her. She will become insane if she doesn't go to Sambalpur. Sir, on that day, you agreed to Goura's transfer.

The story ended, but he felt uncomfortable. The head assistant spoke more like a politician rather than requesting him. The guy convinced him regarding Gourang and his sister-in-law though he had never seen anyone of them. In the meantime, the peon, an unknown face to him, entered the room with the lunchbox. He got an opportunity to stop the conversation.

- Hello!

- Sir, I have kept the file ready with the signature of the Deputy Secretary; waiting for your signature...

- I am going to have my lunch. He disconnected the call.

The lunch wasn't over yet, and the telephone rang. He couldn't understand; what would he say to this head assistant? The conversation was over, and he thought of saying it was the wrong number.

- Hello!

He said very firmly. The call was from the Chief Secretary's office. He has to meet him immediately. He was going to meet him for the first time. He seeks for an appointment three days back.

When he returned from the Chief Secretary's office, his life was utterly changed, and he was elated. He immediately called his wife, Swati.

-Listen! Swati, you will be thrilled to know that the Chief Secretary called me to his office. He spoke to me for more than one and a half hours. He is Mr. Sathe, a Maharashtrian. How does he look? Oh! He is short, bald-headed, fair, has a round face, and wears spectacles. He speaks a lot like you. He talked to me for one and half hours. He also asked me about you; he wanted to know when you would come and has invited me to his house for dinner in the coming Saturday. The most exciting thing is he has taken me as his OSD. I told him that I joined just a week back, and he replied, 'That's an advantage. There is a lot of politics here among the officers. Do you know! From Monday I will sit on the third floor next to his room.

He was still in the trance through. Swati had disconnected the phone. He again lit a cigarette and was wondering about his fate. Fate smiles at people sometimes in his profession. He looked outside. The sunlight was dim. The state was on the eastern border, so the day breaks and evening approaches early, but the house flies between the window, and the curtain isn't as agile as the time. The fly is moving around the limited space.

Right from the beginning, he didn't like the room. The ground floor was crowded with the assistants bicycles. The Chief Secretary told him that a promotee generally fills his present post. What does he have to do with the room? He has got a new posting in a new space. He was ready to go home. From the beginning, when he was posted in Delhi, it was his habit to work from nine to five, irrespective of the workload. According to his routine, he thought of arranging the papers on the table into his briefcase, but there were no papers on his table. There was only a telephone.

He suddenly remembered the head assistant when he saw the telephone. He could imagine those three figures on the other side of the table. The head assistant with a tilak on his forehead and a file in his hand, the sharp, tongued-lady standing behind Gourang Majhi moing forward and saying. 'Excuse me, sir'. But there were no more telephone calls. The head assistant was pleading so much; I think that was the end of the story. He rang the bell, and the peon came and took the empty lunch box.

He stood up and looked through the window. He could see the setting sun rays forming a shady pattern outside and inside the room; he could feel the presence of three shaded images that were looking at him with wide-open eyes. He walked next to them and bid them goodbye. The telephone rang again before he could open the door. He ran towards the phone as quickly as he could.

- Hello! Hello!

His voice was filled with curiosity.

-Sir, there is a lot of chaos

Oh! thank god, it was the head assistant's call.

- Sir, you went for lunch, but Goura didn't listen to me when I told him that you would put your signature in the file on Monday. He howled and screeched in the office. Now, I learnt that he is in the station with his family. He is adamant. At any cost, he will go to Sambalpur today. He is a good guy; the only problem is that he can't leave his sister-in-law, that has made him crazy. Sir, please sign the letter.

He was holding the telephone tightly, and said to himself, 'Don't disconnect the phone because I don't have your number' and added that he was leaving the office for the day.

- I know, Sir.

The Head Assistant's voice chocked

-Sir, Kindly give me only five minutes; I will be there…

- There is no time. Tell me what to do? He asked as if these imaginary shady images present in the room.

-Sir, only your signature…

-Okay, Okay

He became conscious. The formalities of the transfer

had already been completed as the Deputy Secretary had cleared the file. Who will take over the charge? He asked whether the dues were cleared, library books returned, and LTC availed or not.

-Book? Sir, he doesn't know anything other than calculations. No books, all the dues are cleared, and LTC availed. Naidu will take over the charge, that Tamilian, who knows everything in detail.

There is nothing wrong. Everything is appropriately arranged. Let the person go wherever he wants. He has already reached the station; no one will be harmed. Win-win situation. Just a little bit of drama and sudden joy filled with excitement.

- Let him go. I said in a firm voice.

- Will he go, Sir?

The head assistant was filled with joy

- Sir, you are like God. Goura is lucky. I will be there in a few seconds.

- Not necessary

- And the file?

- Write in that file… He became more serious

- Write, I have approved. There was a sparkle in *Rangabati's* eyes present in the room

- I will sign on Monday. Let him go first.

Accountant Gourang will begin his new life in Sambalpur irrespective of the allotted department. No one in this room will pick up the phone on Monday. A new episode of life and adjustment will begin on Monday.

When he came out of the room, he was happy, and

there was suave in his gait. The corridor was empty as the assistants had already left on their bicycles. Searching for the cigarette packet. he put his hand in the pocket. Suddenly he could recall that he had thrown the empty cigarette packet in the dustbin; he was startled. He went back to the room quickly. He could neither see those shadows nor the housefly. Why should he leave a proof that he was in that room? He picked up the empty cigarette packet from the dustbin and went out. He is an officer. Even little bit of carelessness from him would not be accepted.

STORY 5

Lilet Dash's Sms

YOU

- Honey! What will you bring for me when you come back from the kitchen (Cochin)?

-Tell me, who will love you like me? You don't understand how lucky you are.

- Ours is a not-so-serious affair. Last year, I became serious without any reason. This year you don't make the mistake

- The earth will look more beautiful if you can find out the right path between truth and hoodwink

- Yes, I know .Even the angels will envy us.

JOKES

-A Quiz. Name a thing which is dry when it goes and becomes wet when it returns?

-Teabags… Haha...

-I am inside your system; how will you delete me?

- Really, I couldn't understand you till now, but who can understand love?

Apan akae sher bolega

Charo taraf chand phek thaila hae light

Bolo to ho gaya hae night

Band kar daaeka light,

Sonae ka tight,

Bolo to a good night

Mere taraf see apko akae puppy,

Apkae friend ko akae puppy ,

Apakae friend Kae friend ko akae puppy ,

Batayen kyun?

Kyun ki ajae maera doggy nae dus puppy ko Janam Diya hai…!

-Without love, days are sad days, days of mouring, teary days, worse days, thirsty days, frightful days, shattered days. Do fall in love…happy Valentine's Day.

-There is no scarcity of people who flirt in this world. Look at the sun; it comes in the morning with *Usha*, the whole day stays with *Kiran* and goes back with *Sandhya*.

YOU

-I want to thank you for everything, even for the grief, which pushed me to the other part; Good, I also learnt a lesson in life

-The truth is, I love her as much as she loves me. You have never given me enough time and attention, of course, it's not a matter to be discussed today.

-Is it the last thing in love to only look intensely at others?

-According to me, you have given me your body, but not your soul. I could understand what I didn't get on New Year's eve.

- You taught me to lie, you taught me how to drink coffee with rum, you called me for the first time, and you brought me on this untrodden path.

FOREIGN

-I was in a hotel in Geneva. On one side of the hotel was the panoramic view of the Swiss Alps, and on the other side was a lake where the white swans were drifting on the water like small white cotton toys.

-This time, it's pretty cold in Europe. There is snowfall outside. I envisage your presence and the warmth which can turn this winter into a summer solstice.

-This lonely room is veiled with a blanket of slumber. Will you come to wake me up from this slumber?

-Think, only both of us are on the seashore…., inside the pink and white-coloured tent which has puffed up in the air ….leisurely drinking Bacardi.

- If this white puffed balloon douses into the water, what will happen? Wow! We will get drenched.

YOU AND HE

- If she could have loved me, then it would have been something different. If she could have been sensuous, then things would have been different. Am I worthy of being loved! Oh! You can't understand all these.

- Both of you have sabotaged me. I couldn't be close to any one of you.

- Who loves me more? Is it you or he ? Say quickly... asap

- He was the first man in my life, may be because of that, he couldn't realize his responsibility to date.

- Though he was the first man in my life, you are embedded in my soul. How can I forget?

- You will never get (me) as quickly as he got me and still latched on to me.

- He loves me but, I can't get out of you... I am confused...I love both of you...But he is more committed.

OFFER

- *Apun kae bare mae kya socha? Jaldi sochnae ka, kyu ki apan kae pas time bahut kam hae.* (what did you think about me, think fast as we have very less time.

- The offer will end on November 25th. Only one can personally come and avail this offer, and the offer will be authenticated with a kiss.

- I receive others' SMS. Do you envy me for that? You also receive ten thousand freaky SMS, and your demand is increasing,

Abe Bindas bol do ki manjoor hae. (Oh tell me openly that this is acceotable to you)

- I also promise you for the next ten years, this life and youth, *mangata hai to bolo* (if you wish tell me).

- Otherwise, no chance... I love you.

- Why should we think? Still, we have ten more years in our handful of vigor and vitality.

HE AND ME

- To leave everything and elope was my madness. I was testing him. He told me also those things which I wanted to hear.

- Every day, I tell him the same thing, to elope. He could never understand whether I was a storm or a tornado.

- I have given you only one year of my life. You give her one year.

- Nowadays, I fulfill all his desires. But sometimes, if there is a chance to discus about you, then again, we are back to square one…

- Yesterday he came to the airport to receive me, he looked at me intently as if he was scanning me like an ultrasound machine so that could understand me…

- He has kept a surprise for me, by wearing it; it seems I will look like Princess Diana.

- I asked him why he didn't agree to elope with me at that time, he said he would remain ashamed of that matter for the rest of his life.

I, HE, AND YOU (1)

-Yesterday I had a bad dream. I dreamt that three of us drove in a black car towards the riverside. It was going to rain, so both of us went and stood under the tree, and you reversed the vehicle, and while doing so, it fell into the river. I can't say anything more...I was scared and embraced him.

- His chest is covered with hair, and I like the smell of his body. But you don't have hair on your chest...you metro-sexual cheat.

- Have you seen Truffaut's Jules and Jim? I am the same, Catherine, are you scared?

He will come only for me, not for thousands of people like you.

- You are the only obstacle between the two of us...

YOU AND ME (2)

- I showed my sisters the saree which you had gifted me. The elder one appreciated it, and the younger one didn't pay any attention, she felt envious.

- Devdas' father told him to 'leave the house'; mother said 'leave Paro,' and Paro said' leave alcohol'. I am not telling you to leave me...

- I always long to open your shirt buttons

- I accept that I am wrong, I am on a wrong path, I don't have any power to decide.

- *Uncle ji pahunch gaye kya? Aap to bade pahuchae hua niklae..* Hello Uncle, have you reached? You are a conman!

- There are rows of mountains here and a string of Buddhist monasteries...! I have hidden you in my heart among all these.

- I expected just a little from you, not much.

- Aerodynamically, the bumblebee should not be able to fly. But the bumblebee does not know it, so it goes flying anyway! Similarly our love…

- I am going to take a bath. Think…

ONLY ME

On March 18th, at 10.45 A.M., I took a vow that I would never change my mind.

- I vouch for being with you and giving shape to our imaginations.

- It's challenging to understand known people, but I can understand an unknown person much better.

Half of the people are after me in this city, and the rest don't understand what they are missing…

- The rain here is as sensual as the nights in Paris.

- Oh! This continuous rain! I feel like a sleeping net to you.

- There is very little time and more appreciators. What will I do?

- My sister-in-law doubts and envies me. How many of them have a good fate to fall in love with two respectable persons?

- Now I am insane.

ONLY YOU

- Do you remember? Once I challenged you in the car when we stopped near the Zebra crossing to kiss me irrespective of others'noticing this. You kissed me. Where is that courage now?

- You are a sick-minded, middle-class lover like the tenants of Cuttack who reside in a house, don't pay the rent, are reluctant to leave, and while leaving, spoil the house and go.

- *Kuch to hae baat aap main*...(There is something special about you)

YOU AND HE

- If you meet that person who loved me once, tell him that from this New Year, I will not be alone

- Oh! finally, you both met? What did you discuss about me? You will also not say anything! I am waiting for his SMS.

- Oh! Were there no fireworks? I thought both of you would come to exchange blows...

- Regarding our relationship, you will score 3/10, and he will score 7/10; still he isn't satisfied. Some people are too cocksure! There is no limitation for love...

- He has excused me many a times. Now it's time for me to forgive you.

- Otherwise, next time, I will love a bully who will beat both of you black and blue.

SOUTH

- I have come to your city for a few days. If we meet it's ok, otherwise it doesn't really matter.

- I am fine and can do things on my own.(even now also, can do things on my own)

- You try to convince your boss. I can be on the lap, dance on his table, and do anything, but you try to come…

- If you don't come at the earliest, remember, I may change my mind.

- At this place in the south, it's too hot; I don't feel like wearing anything, and if you come, what's the necessity for that?

- In the last few years, I have lost the inclination towards emotional necessity. But, this southern cityon the seashore has turned me into a dangerous weapon. Who is responsible for that? The weather of this place or it is me who doesn't understand the language…

- I have seen lust in your eyes, Felt the ecstasy in your arms. I didn't forget anything…

- Remember, I am like a man-eater tigress living in this southern part of India… come at your own risk…

ONLY HE

- I love him and will return to him as he is my first love.

- This is the last chance for me, and he has enough time.

- If he wouldn't have been there, then I wouldn't have exited.'

- He has promised me that he will come. I don't know when my love will play hide and seek with me …

- Guys, what am I doing now?

- I always defeated him in games of scrabble. How? I cheat…

- It's normal for you and me, we always fight and then make up but I told him once, which ignited a fire.

HE, YOU, AND ME (1)

- Did you call me from an unknown number?

- I am busy with my other work though I love you.

- The time limit of my love for someone is only a year, except you…

- I have not forgotten you, just to prove that my love for you wasn't a child's play.

I never wanted a firm commitment from you, especially from you.

- Monsoon will arrive by the end of June, and I will be alone here. Hey! My only non-platonic friend, will you come?

- *Mausam akaedam hit, aur tabiyat bhi fit, To chale kya Khandala?* (the weather is right, and my health us, should we go to Khandala

- I am obsessed with you…

- What's the definition of our relationship? I can't answer, nor can you

- This message was read to someone who loves or hates or wants to kill…Think! Why did I forward you the message?

HE, YOU, AND ME (2)

- It's my ill fate that both of you are in the same City. Don't mind please, I will call him first after I reach.

- I will meet both of you. Then we will decide…My love is pining for me…tell me, what should I do?

- No, I have changed my mind; I will never meet him…

- I don't know who is he…

- I told him that you had come and I met you socially in Ranga Swami's house. Nowadays, I can speak nonstop lies.

I didn't tell him that you will come; don't tell him if he asks.

- Why didn't he call me for so many days? Now let him wait... this is my wish.

- Last year, when I was going through a tough time in my life, he was with me, not you. So you shut up…

PHILOSOPHY OF LIFE

- Behind every successful man, there is a woman, and behind every satisfied woman, there is a tired man (on the bed) … Ha…ha…

What is the last thing in love, in intensely staring at someone

-I get immense pleasure when someone looks at me and touches me…touch wood….

-You wanted, and you got. It's your fate. You wanted

and waited; it's an opportunity, you compromised; it's life and love.

-I have learned to be silent from noisy people, learnt to be patient with impatience, and learnt to be thankful to thankless people.

- We will together find a way, or make one…

-I don't have any more interest in love or poetry… I am into trade- unionism these days…

-A river flows in my heart….

-I think love is the greatest lie, and I am tired of this lie. I'm tired of lying for 100 times.

The Attire

(THE STORY OF A TAILOR)

I am conscious of my attire; maybe it's in my blood. Even when my father was finically hardpressed he wore a bright white dhoti, white or brown linen kurta, a pair of Bata sandals, and a rectangular dial wristwatch. When we came to Cuttack from our village in 1950, my father had taken a house on rent from Mr. Ramaachandra Dhala in *Kigali, Dhammapada*. It was a thatch roof, one-room house but very neat and clean.

The bed was properly arranged with a clean bed sheet. The table was covered with a cloth. On it was placed a set of books by *Shakespeare, George Bernard Shaw, Mansingh, Sachi Routray, Gyanendra Burma, Arthur Miller, and Noel Peirce Coward*. On the first day of our arrival in the night, my mother and sister spread the rug and slept on the floor. After we arrived that afternoon from the village riding the small match stick-sized bus, spoiling the neatly arranged bed , *Jhuni* and I danced and played on the bed.

The school dress and shoes were effortless, but I looked at the grey-blue uniform of Stewart school with rapaciousness. In our Collegiate school, there was no such uniform. While studying in school for the first time, I developed an affinity towards clothes because of my friend Bikas Mohanty. I envied him. He belonged to a renowned doctor's family. Once he came wearing a calendar shirt, which we referred to as Hawai shirt, on which the calendar of the year was printed. In our class, there were few girls. I became more envious when a few of them went and stood next to Bikas to read the printed calendar on his shirt. Once to compete with Bikas, I borrowed the beret from one of my distant cousin, a police constable in the village, and wore it to school. No one paid attention to it. Of course, one of my friends commented me as a 'spectacle-wearing monkey.'

My father bought an electric iron from the GEC showroom in Kolkata on his way back after the cinema shooting of 'Sri Jagannath.'That became a symbol of status among the tenants of the rented house in the locality. Still there was no electricity connection, just an amalgamation of thatched and pukka cottages. But we weren't baffled by that. Although the method wasn't fruitful, Jhuni and I tried to iron our clean school uniform on the table with a cold iron and folded it.

Within a few years, Raj Kapoor's film 'Awara' was released . The film was a hit and taking advantage of that, one of the companies named a readymade shirt as 'Awara shirt' and started selling it. The small logo of RK Production was printed on the yellow cloth with Nargis and Raj Kapoor close to each other; Raj Kapoor holding a guitar in his hand, leaning towards Nargis.

I wanted that 'Awara shirt' for *Ganesh Puja* at any cost and threw tantrums at home. My parents discussed and concluded that the child would go astray by wearing this type of cheap designed shirt. On the day of Ganesh Puja, I didn't wear anything new; I was naked, cried bitterly, and slept on the bed upside down. To annoy my mother, I chewed a handful of boiled rice kept in a sack to spoil the puja rituals. My mother also took revenge on me; she called the two sisters, Japan and Germany (May be born during World War II), and told that I had invited them to our house; brought them to the room where I was lying stark naked in anger.

At that time, 'Awara Shirt' was available in the *Jayanarayan* Cloth store situated at *Marwadi Pati*. Bhubaneswar had no existenc at that time. In that store, for the first time in Odisha, a mannequin draped in a saree was displayed. My father went to that store, but instead of purchasing that shiny yellow shirt, by paying more money, he bought a thick grey color shirt. It seemed like the tunic which was going to be used by the Communist Party of the Soviet Union's twentieth session. I still think about my parent's injustice. Whatever bad was supposed to happen in life has happened. Could anyone stop it? Yet, I couldn't wear that 'Awara shirt.'

Custom-made tailored clothes are more expensive than the readymade garments available in western stores. In London's 'Syavhail Row,' tailor-made suits are available, which are pretty costly. But, at that time, the readymade shirts available at Cuttack's Jayanarayan Kedarnath was more expensive than tailor-made shirts, and they didn't fit into size. That's why we started searching for a tailor. 'Bombay Tailoring Shop' was very famous during my school days, and a calm and composed Muslim guy was the shop's owner. One could see a measuring tape around his shoulder all the time, just like the doctors keep their stethoscopes. The shop was situated in *Chunibhati lane*, and I had never seen this man with a smile, but the label 'Bombay Tailoring' sewed to the shirt's collar was enough to stimulate my interest in the garments.

During my college days, the store 'L'Myaginifico,' which opened between *Mani Sahu Square* and *Mangalabagh,* brought a revolutionary change in the history of tailor-made garments. This type of name was rare in Cuttack and came with high stitching charges. The joint directors of this agency were two young men, *Bibek and Buna Panda.* This agency came into the form based on the experience of one of them who visited Singapore. There were lots of gossip about *Buna Panda's* motorcycle and his thrilling personality. After meeting a girl in the Puri sea beach, *Buna Panda,* on his bike, raced agianst the Kolkata bound train and dated her thrice at the Puri, Bhubaneswar, and Cuttack stations. Akshaya Mohanty, who took lots of interest in this issue, wrote about this episode and published it in a festival series.

Babu Bhai tailor in Buxibazar stitched my clothes regularly. It was situated near to my regular pan shop, and *Babu Bhai* liked me because I wrote poems. In reality, *Babu Bhai* was more of a saint and a musician in the true sense than just a tailor. He composed the prayer songs of Jesus Christ and played the harmonium perfectly. In brief, after closing his shop, he used to take out his harmonium, sit in his shop, and sing the songs that filled the air with pain and compassion. During Christmas, competitions were held between the Christian communities, and *Babu Bhai* organized these competitions. Akshaya Mohanty and I composed songs for him based on the thorn-crowned Jesus Christ, filled with pain and compassion. The music was written with the same tune as the super hit song *'Sabi, Sabi..'*

Once, I asked *Babu Bhai* why did the tailors take so much time to stitch. If you gave something for stitching during that year's *Dushera*, you might expect it to get during the next *Dushera. Babu Bhai* silently brought a cloth, marked it with chalk, cut it accordingly, and stitched it. It took him only forty-five minutes to sew the pant, excluding stitching buttons.

I learnt a few words related to tailoring like button stitch, lining, *buckram*, mending, *bakhya*, double stitch, etc. There were a few problems associated with stitching, like if the '*Bukram*' wasn't good and not imported one, then the collar wouldn't set correctly. Other questions like how much would the *mahuri* of the pant be, would there be pleats near the waist, what would be the design at the back of the shirt, would there be a flap over the pocket and strap on the shoulders. Fashion changes with time. What was happening in London and Paris was not known in Cuttack; only *Babu Bhai* tailor could say that, and we blindly followed him as the players of a football match followed the referee's decision. Of course, when the Bobby film-type bell button trousers and the polka-dotted shirt were introduced in the market, I had already left Cuttack.

Who isn't eager to know about the women's garments? I was willing to learn. *Prafulla tailor* in our area was known for stitching blouses, dresses, and saree falls. Sometimes he used to stitch a pair of pillow covers for us, when my father insisted. His shop was situated on a narrow corridor and in the evening was crowded with ladies. He used to take measurement for each of them one by one and drew a curtain while taking the measure. I became anxious when I saw a few of my classmates there. I left the city for a few years for working somewhere else. When I returned, I noticed that the narrow corridor still existed, but there was no sign of the tailoring shop, and in that place a homeopathic shop had opened. The doctor was none other than *Prafulla tailor*. Instead of the measuring tape, a stethoscope was hanging around his neck, and many wealthy *Marwadi* ladies were crowded over there.

I still remember him taking measurement of the girls. Who knows, maybe the tailor was responsible for that! I have mentioned this in one of my poems,. Once upon a time, this poem was the talk of the town. A few days back, there was a dinner gathering in Salt Lake, Kolkata. When the group became a little unruly, one of my friends asked me if I was still writing those filthy poems? He was indicating towards that old poem *'Mahumachi'* (Honey Bee) where there was a mention about the young, adolescent girl Baby.

In that gathering at Salt Lake, there were many young, educated, and elite girls. One of them suddenly said may be the tailor is *Pradip da* of Salt Lake. Someone else said that if he took clothes for stitching during Dushera, he returned them during *Pohili Baisakhi* (The first month of summer). A lady had once said, 'Listen, *Pradipda,* so many ladies come to your shop, why don't you arrange for curtains?' *Pradipda* replied, 'Whatever I do, I do in the open, not behind the curtains.' A gentleman commented that he had put up a signboard in front of his shop, mentioning, 'In this shop, nothing can be done flawlessly. Come at your own risk'. Still, the place was crowded. Another hefty girl said he made the kurta so tight-fitting that it was difficult for her to breathe. She told him, 'Pradipda, please open the stitch and increase a few inches.' He looked at her angrily and said, 'I will only be increasing; why can't you decrease'? She felt like being strangulating.

In the meantime, a tall dusky young girl came forward and said that she took her sister in law who stays in Mumbai, to *Pradipda's* shop during last puja. *Pradipda* looked at her and said, 'Are you associated with the Mumbai film industry?' My sister-in-law laughed and said 'no'. *Pradipda* then said, 'Indeed, you look like a Mumbai film heroine's mother.' My sister-in-law, who is a bit hefty, returned home and cried. *Hemantada's* daughter Lipsa, a student of Presidency College, doing her MA in English, spoke into my ears and said, 'Do you know how bad-mannered is *Pradipda*? My mother wanted to make an appointment to take my measurements, and *Pradipda* said, 'Not necessary, I have seen her since her childhood, I know her measurements.'

In Kolkata, a discussion can never end without a political debate. In the meantime, an elderly man said, 'Did you see *Trinamul Congress* poster in *Pradip*'s shop?' He had spent thirty years with CPM and now has changed his party to know about prospects. Another middle-aged lady laughed and said, 'Yes, we know. He had taken the measurement of a *Trinamul Congress* MLA's wife in a party letterhead and had pasted it on his cupboard. Whoever comes to his shop reads it.' Suddenly a little girl made everyone quiet and said, '*Pradipda* is a very good person. Last year when my dog Jackey died, at that time, *Pradipda* left his shop and came; he consoled my father. He dug the grave in our garden to bury Jackey.'

The pride of a tailor depends on his skills and expertise but, when that gets mixed up with his speaking skills, he becomes incomparable. Once, I read in a book regarding a customer who was pissed off; he said, 'It's almost one and a half months, my trousers are still not ready. Do you know or not, God created this world in seven days.' The tailor took out his newly stitched trouser, opened it in front of him, and said sarcastically, 'Look at the trouser that I made and look at the world created by God and tell which is flawless?'

The Interview

Namaskar! My name is Sonia. My father's name is Prafulla Mahapatra. He works as a professor in the university. Last year I completed my bachelor's degree with philosophy honours. At present, I am not doing anything.

It's not that only for my father I studied Philosophy. I liked the subject. I knew that there weren't many opportunities available if I take philosophy; this is my first attempt to get a job.

I never thought about what would I get reading philosophy? Sometimes I wonder, what did life give to the old widow lady *Nilaa* who stays in the *Abadhuta Matha* near Bindusagar? Or my neighbor *Bijayaa Apa* (sister) who spends all her holidays correcting student's answer scripts and reluctant to demand anything from life?

There is no specific time when these thoughts come to my mind. I was a little bit naughty during my childhood. My mother would take me to terrace of our single-storied rented house in the evening and tell me to sit quietly, pointing towards the stars in the sky. Absentmindedly, I used to sit quietly gazing the stars. But presently, when I go through the Star Dust magazine, randowm thoughts creep into my mind.

Sir, are you going to ask me questions now? You

may ask. Oh! Is it the question, what's the population of India? Sir, the people of India, are uncountable. The word 'uncountable' is so interesting. It makes the answer simple for many difficult questions. The stars in the sky, the raindrops, the leaves on the trees, and India's population are all uncountable. This word itself makes things obvious. It's not a big thing to tell just a number. Sir, whatever may be India's population, you can't do anything about it. Can you reduce India's population?

What did you ask, Sir? Rio de Janerio? Is this the name of any animal? Oh! Rio, where a few days back earth summit was held? I understood, Sir. You are asking me how to protect the environment? Sir, kindly tell me how it can be done. In *Pratap Bhai*'s school, just five days back, they fell a huge tree to construct the staff quarters. Listen to me, Sir, if trees and forests are destroyed, human beings may perish, but if human beings live, then surely everything will perish, including trees and forests.

If fewer human beings can be reduced and more and more trees cover the place, it will be awesome, Sir. I have seen how near to my house, branches of the tree have grown longer to cover the old temple completely. Similarly, I hope the trees and the forests could engulf Cuttack and Bhubaneswar! Suppose right from *Rasulgarh* till *Kalinga Studio* everything can turn into a forest. All the buildings, water tanks, temples could get covered by forest, and only the tip of the Lingaraj temple or the edifice of Vanivihar library could only be seen. People would have carried an axe with them to clear their way through the bushes and protected themselves from the python on their way while visiting the secretariat. If near the market at noon, one could hear the fierce roar or peacocks consoling the patients near a hospital window. The forest could engulf the police station, market, secretariat, governor's house, and everything. The flights can be seen searching for the airport hovering over the forest, and Cuttack would have been only a forest and two rivers around: *Mahanadi* and *Kathjodi*.

What did you ask, Sir? What kind of job do I like? Do you have any job where I can cry silently? I love riding a bicycle in the lane near to the temple. Do you have a position for this type of job? Listen! Sir, when Rahul rides his motorcycle dressed smartly, wearing sunglasses, I love to watch him. Nowadays, standing on the terrace, my job is to protect him though I am unpaid for this job.

Leave it, sir; what's the meaning of just attending an interview? You know it very well that I won't get this job. Are you asking me why I came to participate in the discussion? To be very truthful, I have come in search of myself. Are you laughing? There is one more important reason which I don't want but will tell you. I just now told you about my present job of staring at Rahul whenever he goes out on his motorcycle; in that matter, there is a problem; I have never spoken to Rahul nor met him. I just love looking at him from a distance. I have seen a girl sitting behind him in his motorcycle for the past few days. She also wears sunglasses. Both go to Rahul's house, and Rahul plays music that I can hear. After some time, they leave the house. I don't know that girl's name, but I can't tolerate it when I see them together. I thought I would lose that job very soon and told myself, why commit suicide? It's better to attend this interview. *Bijaya Apa* will now think that I am getting mature.

Really Sir, when I was not born, this world existed; if I am not there, then this world will exist, so why will anyone be bothered about my existence?

What did you say, Sir? Last question? You may ask. What's the weight of the moon? My God! until now, not even the Sun has asked this question, then why are you asking? How is someone bothered about the weight of the moon! Sir, I really can't tell you the importance of the moon. Still, I think the moon doesn't have weight. Have you ever seen the moon? It is weightless as it travels so swiftly through the clouds, and if it has weight, I think that will be lesser than the weight of your bald head !

The Circle

There was still pain in the backbone. *Appa Rao* made a gesture of standing by the bicycle and stretched his body. A Few people came from the crowd, peeping like a tortoise from its shell, thinking as if some stunt was being shown.

Appa Rao is a mix of anger and sympathy. Hey! The troubled souls, doesn't trick exist everywhere? There is a trick in the bar, on the dancing hall, in love, and in the interview. Appa Rao increased the speed to show a few of his stunts on the bicycle though he had a sharp pain in his backbone.

It was a clear blue sky; the rays were brilliantly red and orange. It was a bold, brilliant, and rich sunset. There was a similarity between the clear blue sky and Soumya;s doe-eyed eyes. Somehow Appa Rao could muster his courage.

Whenever he thought about Soumya, he felt self-centered and something runs through his subconscious mind. Today he is frequently remembering her. Why does he remember her so often while crying?

Appa Rao couldn't get an appropriate answer to his question. Soumya liked the way he rode the bicycle. She applauded whenever he stood first on the cycling race during college sports day. Soumya was thrilled by the speed and whirl he displayed on his bike. No one knew the reasons for showing so uch interest. That's why even after a breakup with Soumya, he tried to master the craft for his livelihood. He had an adorable mother and lots of landed property in Ernakulum. Appa Roa still needs to remember that. He shows the stunt on the bicycle as Soumya loved it and would have done any petty jobs if Soumya would have enjoyed doing even boot polishing.

Jimutabahana came.

-What happened?

- Show a stunt… There is a request.

- Please, I can't do. Appa Rao suddenly felt irritated. Like a small child without giving a second thought, very often he gets angry.

Jimutabahana has lots of patience.

Appa Rao suddenly changed his speed and reached the centrum of the ground. Appa Rao will complete ninety-six hours in the next 4 and 14 minutes and win twenty-five thousand rupees. God is great…..

Appa Rao got ready to show his stunts. He has taken five thousand rupees in advance from the city citizen counsel after signing a bond. The son of a businessman has a bet of five thousand rupees on him. He has sold himself to entertain others.

Appa Rao walked towards the stage. Jimutabahana was there

The first person to welcome him to the city was this Jimutabahana. He did the publicity, printed the placards, and obtained permission from the authority. He publicized the arrival of Appa Rao with the help of a few young volunteers on a horse cart with a loudspeaker. Almost ninety-two hours back, a Deputy Minister had inaugurated the opening ceremony of the event ....

He started showing his stunts despite acute pain on the calf muscle. He had learned these tricks from a circus. The six feet tall Appa Rao was horizontal on the bicycle, caught hold of the paddle with his hands, and drove it; it was really fascinating.

Soumya liked this stunt of Appa Rao. He increased his speed and went around like a whirlpool.

Oh! Maybe he would have fallen as the bicycle slipped. Jimutabahana stood up on the stage in fear. If Appa Rao would fall, he would have lost a few thousand rupees.... Jimutabahana thanked God.

Soumya was a student in his sixth year studying Mathematics. She had changed her subject from Philosophy to Mathematics a few years back.No one knows why. Appa Rao was a student in the fourth year studying History. That way, Soumya was two years senior to him though Appa Rao had failed in his B.A. final examination.

Who is older to whom is still unknown, then how come they fell in love? What could be the answer to this question? There is no such calculation in love,like for a student of Mathematics, Soumya knew very well that there was no specific method to solve this sum. Appa Rao also knew that it would have taken a different course if the love had been one-sided.

Appa Rao looked at the sky, as dark as his fate. He dreamt of a house, being a husband, a father, owning coconut groves in Ernakulum by the sea.

The day Appa Rao failed to qualify in the examination,

he took a long ride in Madras's quiet and clean roads on his bicycle and rertuned back after a while. Soumya was waiting for him as she knew about his result. He kept his hands on her shoulder and asked, 'Will you hate me?' Holding his hands, Soumya laughed, and replied,' How is history related to me'?

Someone was whistling loudly; Jimutabahana was quarreling with someone on the stage.

Appa Rao was very agile on that day. Meanwhile, he had mastered history. Soumya glanced at him with deeper warmth and earnestness. He immediately handed over a letter to Soumya. Before she could finish reading the letter, he pulled her towards a group of friends. Soumya didn't retaliate; instead asked him a question:

-Should I select the girl?

-What do you mean ! (Appa Rao asked in apprehension)

- Let me find out about your preferemces. Which type of girl are you interested in?

Soumya had a mystique smile on her lips- like a puzzle for Appa Rao. He looked at her in astonishment

Soumya turned relatively normal and said:

-Your mother has mentioned in the letter regarding your marriage. Will it be according to my choice?

-Oh! you know how to speak well…

-It's not like that. Don't you have your own choice and preference?

- Yes, You

-No

A sudden change in Soumya's tone changed the air. There was a heaviness in her tone.

-Excuse me, Naresh

-Means?

Appa Rao was apprehensive and asked

-No, no I ….

- I…?

- I can't marry you.

Sowmya responded contemplating

-Naresh, I can't marry you because I love you. I can't limit this relationship to a name.

Appa Rao couldn't understand the exact connotation of what Soumya said; It was too complicated for him to understand.

-Soumya….. You….

Even if he tried to, he could not pass a derogatory word like 'whore' or 'fallen women' to her. After that, the matter of contention was obvious.

After a few days, while spending a nomadic life in a railway station shed, he came across a photograph printed on a page of Illustrated Weekly. Among the pictures of the newly married couples, he saw the photo of Soumya with her doctor husband. Appa Rao looked carefully at the photograph. Soumya looked older than her husband.

Then?

The bottom line is Soumya was her friend, philosopher, and guide; maybe she never thought to confine the relationship to the appellation of a wife.

There was a show after forty five minutes. People have already started assembling. A few constables in their red turbans were also present and they looked like the rooster's wattle. There was melancholy in the air and the bright, sparkling light on the road.

I hope Appa Rao isn't dreaming.

He wiped his eyes on his palm and looked. What a surprise! The same features, bright eyes, and hair plaits decorated with flowers.

Was she Soumya?

Soumya couldn't be present as she stayed a few hundred miles away. She wasn't a ghost who would appear suddenly.

Who was she?

The girl was quite cheerful and was twittering with her friends.

Appa Rao went up and down many times. Their eyes met every time. The girl left the place.

Of course! The girl wasn't Soumya but a look-alike.

Passion that interred in his bones for many years ultimately took shape, and he decided immediately to win over the girl.

He knew that he was an unknown sportsman and the girl was like a mirage.

The girl had left. She had the same attitude as Soumya. He felt as if Soumya was leaving the place. Just a few minutes, and she would be away. But he made up his mind to win that girl.

Soumya was like a deep blue ocean. She had rejected the marriage proposal as mere acceptance would have made it like narrow spectrum for her. But tonight will transcend the boundaries- a night filled with desire.

The girl was walking away, and Soumya's fond memories were creeping in. It was hardly a matter of a few minutes to reach the road as the exit gate was nearby.

Soumya loved him, so she didn't marry. Maybe she married someone else whom she didn't....

Appa Rao was restless. The memories blurred his vision.

Soumya was now in a vicious circle. She too appeared aged with dark circles underneath eyes, similar to the photograph in the Illustrated Weekly.

He could see Soumya holding his hands on the bicycle handle and asking him, 'Naresh, which type of girl do you want? You must be having a preference.'

Appa Rao fell down from the bicycle in agony. Jimutabhana stood stunned on the stage. Appa Rao fell from his bicycle just ten minutes before the stipulated time.

STORY 9

Alice's Mother

'You don't have any morality as far as women are concerned; we all know this very well, but to chase older ladies throughout your life, what type of psychology is this? One cannot understand .' Ramesh said, pouring water into the whisky glass.

I answered back, 'Which type of cocktail are you making by mixing water instead of soda into whiskey'?

Leave it! I have already stopped using soda nearly fifteen years back. I added half soda to the whiskey in days gone by, and now I add only water.

But, brother! I can manage without whisky but not without soda.

'In a similar way as you hanker for old women,' said Ramesh.

All of them burst into laughter. Again 'older women' became a topic for discussion in that seaside, old house which had been renovated recently. The bountiful sea could be seen from the house earlier, but now,after the restoration, the view was obstructed by the stretch of star hotels constructed in that area. It was raining like cats and dogs, so the sound made by the sea was also not heard.

I had come to that city just for a day, and the flight got

canceled due to bad weather. I had spent my childhood in this city, but there was no other way to stay in a hotel that day. A few old friends hauled me to this club. The reason for this charge was Mrs. ManoRamaa Rao, who accompanied me to this temple city to participate in an archaeological seminar. She had a voluptuous physique and was youthful at the age of fifty. She dropped me in this club on her way to the workshop. My friends observed it, and it became a topic for discussion.

My relationship with Mrs.Rao was only limited to wishing her. We stayed in different hotels, and our destination was different. I didn't contradict Ramesh that day because he knows a few of my old secrets and loses control over his tongue when drunk. At that moment, Binayak entered. He had taken voluntary retirement from his job, joined a political party as the secretary, and now avoids drinking in public or a club. The argument took a different turn, and the topic was about hypocrites.

It had been raining continuously, and with the approaching night, it increased in intensity. Our table was full of empty glasses by this time, and no one was interested in having dinner. I returned to the hotel. I stood on the balcony and smoked. The rainfall increased, and hardly any vehicle could be seen on the road. The existence of the sea could be felt from the moist air. While standing in the darkness of the balcony, I suddenly remembered the argument on my inclination towards older women for which Ramesh had humiliated me. I thought I should have mentioned the book 'In Praise of Older Women ' to him. I suddenly remembered the photograph of Mae West and Sophia Loren in their older age. I was also eager to see Suchitra Sen at least once, who avoids appearing in the general public at this age.

The concern about older ladies again engrossed me. Ramesh was right; I couldn't get out of the fascination and lust for the older women and their aging bodies) What could be the reason? I lit the third cigarette and anticipated,' Were they more mature and experienced in presenting their bodies'? Or did distancing generate allurement? or did distancing, as in every case, ehnaced their allurement That dark and rainy night reminded me of an incident that had happened nearly forty years back in a Christian household of the city in broad daylight. That incident had initiated the spark within me and the attraction towards older ladies. I came down from the balcony and tried to identify the place .I reached the place. I could hear the barking of a pack of dogs, which is a roundabout way indicated that I was right.

The city was different forty years back. It was thinly populated; people's attire was different, and so was the road, which remained empty because of the few vehicles. Everything seemed to be ethereal, the vast spread of sand near the seashore, the happy gang of hippies smoking weeds, and the white foam on the water. The daintiest was Alice's blonde hair, which drifted in the air like a golden thread, tangling and untangling as she sat under the fan in the classroom or walked along the seashore. Alice looked like a fairy from Hans Andersen's fairy tales. She inherited the look from her Anglo-Indian mother.

In the city, near the station where the narrow meter-gauge railway line ended, a small colony of Christian settlement existed for a long time. There were only remains of the colony after forty years, and I wasn't anxious to walk around that place. I remembered Alice's long courtyard, which divided the house into the living room and the bedroom. On the backside, there was a kitchen, storeroom, and bathroom. A broad red porch connected the room on one side of the courtyard, which had a corrugated tin roof.

Alice was my classmate in the fourth standard, so I had access to her house. On my first visit to the Christian settlement, I understood that their way of living and culture differed from ours. There was an old church in the middle of the colony. The roads were constructed differently. There was a difference in our and their culture. Like, there might or might not be a gate m, but there was a garden in the front of the house, curtains on the window, a framed wall hanging on which w 'Love is God' was written, a gramophone, cigarette, many English books on the rack, and tea in a cup.

Alice belonged to a lower-middle-class family; therefore, there was neither a boundary wall nor a calling bell in their house. The door opened into the room, which had a bed, chairs for sitting, a study table, and her father's bicycle, which was kept there at night. Alice's father, James Mohanty, was a driver in Railways, but as he fell sick and couldn't walk correctly, he switched over and started working in the Railway canteen. Her grandmother had expired. Her photograph was framed and kept in the room with a crepe paper garland. Alice had two brothers, Freddy and Hirak, and they studied in different grades in the same school.

Alice's mother was the most beautiful lady in the house. Alice addressed her father as' Daddy', a converted Christian who was from the village but addressed her mother as 'Bou,' an Anglo Indian. I still couldn't understand the mystery behind it. The word 'Bou' shows a different entity in Odia, like a weak and timid lady, but Alice's mother contradicted that image. She was slender, tall, fair-skinned, had sharp & defined facial features, and lovely expressive brown eyes. Generally, the Europeans look fair and pale, but she has dark black hair and a radiant personality. I was awestruck when I saw her for the first time and appreciated her full-lipped enchanting smile.

In front of Alice's mother, James Mohanty looked like an ugly duck, but he was hardly seen with his wife. At that age, I didn't know about their relationship, and I could only perceive his ugly face. After many years I remembered James Mohanty while watching the film 'Bhumika' starring Smita Patel and Amol Palekar; I could relate Amol Palekar, who was more of a broker than a husband with James Mohanty. He limped, had a bout of cough, and looked shabby like a deserted boat in the seashore. In contrast, Alice's mother was like a beautiful ship gliding through the waves, charming and fascinating.

Alice was a miniature replica of her mother, but the sons were like their father, dusky, unkempt but healthier than James Mohanty. I could make out that I was inclined towards Alice as I dreamt of her in my dreams, and the next day when I would meet her in the school, I would feel ashamed of myself. At that immature age, there was no restriction for meeting either from the school side or the parents, but she was encompassed by many other boys at school, which I didn't like. The safest place was Alice's courtyard, where most of the time, we were left alone by her brothers while playing. I eagerly waited for that joyful moment every day after school.

I was aware of the regular household activities of Alice's house. Instead of going home, I went to Alice's house from school with my school bag. We played together in the long courtyard till evening. I could notice Alice's mother taking a bath in the evening, wearing fresh clothes, and dressing up. She looked splendid. I couldn't trust my eyes and would think,' Is there any other mother on earth who is as beautiful as her'?

I could not tolerate it when a man named Chaturbhuja Pujapanda, who was a healthy, fair, and robust, young man came to their house riding a Bullet motorcycle. Whenever he came, James Mohanty, who hardly spoke, would become loquacious, children would run around him in excitement, shouting 'Panda uncle- Panda uncle', and a full-lipped smile and contentment would mirror on Alice's mother's face. Everything would become normal after some time, but I couldn't endure the exchange of the intoxicating glance between them and the shyness in Alice's mother's face. As a result, instead of dreaming about Alice, I dreamt about her mother, imagining her as the pretty lady in the Nirma washing powder and the Lyril soap advertisement. Towards the dawn, I dreamt about Chaturbhuja Pujapanda's accident and wished it could be true!

My imagination took a new twist when we conceived a play to spend time in Alice's house during the Makar Sankranti holidays. There was a scene in the play called 'Daddy Mummy.' Fredrick was the play's director and also the leading actor, the home-ruler or the 'daddy.' Gayatri Jha, a Bihari girl, and a neighbor was asked to do the role of the ' mummy'. She was studying in our school in the sixth standard. The rehearsal started on Christmas afternoon. Fredrick rode his father's bicycle and came. He kept it leaning against the wall. Gayatri served him lunch, just as a wife serves food to a husband who has come from the office to have his meal. Then they slept on the bed in the drawing-room, and we three (I, Alice, and Hirak) took rest on the outside porch. After some time, Gayatri opened the door suddenly and ran outside towards her house. She sent a message through her sister that she won't act in the play. Fredrick felt embarrassed. Finally, Alice and Hirak went to call Gayatri. I asked Fredrick what had happened. Fredrick didn't answer my question; he raised his shoulder, combed his hair, and walked away from there.

After some time, we all came to the room for a compromise. Fredrick and Hirak tried their best to convenience Gayatri that there was no mistake in the play; Fredrick was not at fault because Panda uncle played this 'Daddy mummy game' with their mother in the afternoon. When the children were too small and were sleeping on the bed, they were brought down from the bed and were made to lie on the rug spread on the floor to make arrangements for Panda uncle. Alice also confessed the same thing to me and told me how she and Hirak tried to play the same game lying on the rug and were scolded by their mother.

I suddenly remembered Chatubhuja Pujapanda riding his Bullet motorcycle on a hot, sweaty summer afternoon. He was a contractor and had his lunch in Alice's house most of the time. He was seen in his fair bare body, wrapped around in the checkered loincloth of James Mohanty, sitting down on the floor of the railing to have his food. Alice's mother fanned him with a palm leaf hand fan. One could see the intimacy reflecting from their eyes. After food, both went to the bedroom and locked themselves in till the sun rays became meager. After that, Chaturbhuja Pujapanda dressed up and left with satisfaction on his face on his Bullet motorcycle. The sound of his motorcycle became intolerable for me. Alice's mother immediately entered the bathroom after he left to refresh herself. James Mohanty returned home late in the evening.

I became acquainted with this repeated story of Alice's house. While convincing Gayatri Jha to play the role, though my importance wasn't vital, it wasn't any less. The rehearsal went well for a few days. Fredrick, the director, also offered me the role of a tuition teacher in the second half. According to the story, after the home-ruler leaves the house, a tuition teacher should come to teach the children and knock at the door. We were busy with the rehearsal, Fredrick wasn't there, and the children were doing their home tasks. Gayatri served me snacks, took me to the bed, and slept next to me . When Fredrick returned, we were under a bed sheet and giggled. Fredrick became angry. He pulled me outside and asked, 'What's going on?'. He said this scene isn't in the play, and how could a tuition teacher sleep with the lady of the house? Gayatri became angry and said that the location should be included in the space as she liked sleeping next to me rather than Fredrick; otherwise, she wouldn't do the play. She left the house. Freddy also left the house with dissatisfaction and irritation. Alice and Hirak went to the ground to watch the kite flying, and I was left alone in the place in an unhappy mood.

I sat on the bed where Gayatri had slept next to me just a few minutes back. 'Did Alice hear what Gayatri said'? This question troubled me. I went to the outside porch and was surprised to see the Bullet of Chaturbhuja Pujapanda parked there. I closed the front door and slowly went to the porch; the white cemented courtyard shone brightly in the sunrays. Alice's bedroom door was closed; only the cooing noise of the pigeon could be heard. I walked without making any noise, crossed the bedroom, and sat under the pole. I was feeling uncomfortable as the rehearsal had stopped in between and was apprehensive regarding the remark of Gayatri as I didn't know what would be the aftereffect of it.

How long did I sit there stretching my legs? I don't remember. Slowly the sunlight was fading, similar to the ray of hope in my heart, and in the sky, I could see a kite flying solo. At that time, I heard the noise of the latch opening. Panda uncle came outside the room dressed appropriately, face smeared with powder, and walked towards the drawing-room tying the band of his wristwatch and said little loudly, 'Children aren't there.' After some time, Alice's mother came outside holding her half draped saree and ran quickly towards the bathroom on the right side of the porch. None of them saw me. No one ever doubted that I was present there. I could hear the sound of the Bullet and the water falling from the tap on the bucket.

The sound of the Bullet bike became fainter with the noise of the children playing outside, but the sound of the water falling on the bucket was louder. I could analyze each sound that I heard. I could listen to the sound made when the bucket was full, the sound of pouring water on the body, falling of the brass pot, washing, rinsing of clothes, and finally, the closing of the tap. Slowly there was silence in the atmosphere. The pigeons were flying back to the parapet. In that brick-and-mortar courtyard, I was the only living being present.

At that moment, the bathroom door opened with a cricking sound. From the entrance, through the courtyard, if a horizontal line were drawn, it would reach the right-left side pole of the porch near the bedroom where I was sitting without anybody's knowledge. Whatever I saw dumbfounded me; thousand alarm bells started ringing on my head. I couldn't stand up, couldn't utter a single word as if I had turned deaf and dumb.

Alice's mother was near the bathroom door, with

her beautiful figure completely nude. She looked like a sculpted marble statue with the reflection of the sunrays. I couldn't take off my eyes from her gorgeous body. The fear inside me liquefied and turned into a deep allurement in a fraction of a second. Before crossing the bathroom threshold, Alice's mother looked around carefully as if she were looking through a telescope to confirm that no one was around. Then she threw back the lock of hair that covered her shoulder and chest. The sunrays reflected from her chest and formed a pattern. She inspected her body from top to bottom, gave a pleasing smile, and started walking. She walked straight and confidently like Eve when Eve had gone to the Garden of Eden to eat the forbidden fruit. There was nothing on her body, not even a hand towel. Though she was swift as a deer, it looked like a snail's paced motion picture where the actress lingered to my lustful eyes.

Alice's mother came to the porch, which joined the two different parts of the house. The closer she came, the better I was able to see her . The drops of water on her body were sparkling like a rhinestone. Maybe she had left the bath towel and her saree in the bedroom. When she was crossing the threshold, I could see her from one side, but when she turned back, we confronted each other. She noticed me. She wasn't prepared for this and screamed. She tried to cover her body with her palm as much as she could. After realizing that it was me, she wanted to make herself comfortable and smiled. Before entering the bedroom, she looked at me, smiled sweetly, and said, 'Bad boy' in a melodious voice. At that time, I became very emotional and thought maybe she was inviting me to her bedroom but suddenly the door closed, and she bolted it from inside.

That specific emotional moment is scripted in my mind forever. That day I left Alice's house immediately. While returning, I was perplexed. I had never seen a completely nude body of a mature woman before. That experience made me feel as if suddenly I had become mature and had crossed the threshold of childhood. Since that day, though Alice requested many times, I stopped visiting her house.

I met Alice's mother a few times as a part of the routine life. She always smiled at me whenever we met but never invited me to visit her house. The play stopped as Gayatri Jha, and stopped going. Years passed, and I left the school and went to college for higher studies. My father also got transferred from that place. After a few years, I got the news that Hirak drowned while swimming near the river mouth, Alice got married and left for Australia, Fredrick worked in Merchant Navy as a sailor, and alcoholic James Mohanty, along with his wife had left the city and got settled in a village near Waltair. There was no news about Chaturbhuja Pujapanda.

I was standing on the balcony of my hotel room and was smoking continuously. I opened a new cigarette packet. It had stopped raining, and dawn was a few hours away. I knew that I couldn't rest as I had to take the morning flight. Still, I couldn't leave the balcony. The key to my attraction towards an older lady, the charm of having a relationship with an older woman, was here in a small courtyard of this city; I couldn't escape from that feeling and allurement. I felt a shiver running down through my body, and the sound of the barking dogs from a far distance backed my imagination.

STORY 10

Possessions

chand tasvīr-e-butāñ chand hasīnoñ ke hutūt
baad marne ke mere ghar se ye sāmāñ niklā

Galib

It was almost 8 p.m. when I died. The young house surgeon first checked my pulse, then used his stethoscope to check my heartbeat, narrowed my eyes with a torch, and finally, when my body didn't respond, annoyed, he looked at his watch and informed the nurse, 8.15 p.m. The nurse wrote something on the paper hanging near my bed. It was a Wednesday, 8 p.m., and the Binaca Geet Mala program had begun, so even if the doctor wouldn't have told the time, I knew the time. Amin Sayani could be heard from the transistor which was either in the fruit shop or medicine shop.

The doctor and the nurse weren't happy with my death because they didn't know me nor my parents. The nurse was South Indian, and the doctor was almost twenty to twenty-five years younger than me. They didn't have any idea about Odia writers. They were badgered by my idle and rude friends from Buxi Bazaar and some of my friends who were writers and news reporters. I felt the duo was in a different mood that day. While taking out the thermometer from my mouth, they touched each other. When both of them took their hands to bring the thermometer, the doctor held the hand of the nurse and said, 'Your hands are so cold,' and the nurse slowly took her hand away.

The doctor looked at the thermometer under the light. The mercury had crossed the line. The doctor thought for a moment that I might die and gave a mischievous look at (to) the nurse. The nurse (dusky and not fluent in Odia) gave a flirtatious glance at the young doctor and moved around the medicine cupboard like a merry go round. The doctor stood straight with one hand in his pocket, and with the other, he fiddled with his hair. He kept his palm on my burning forehead. He touched the nurse with his warm palm and said, 'Look how hot are my palm and my entire body? The nurse kept her fingers on her lips and said, 'Keep quiet! Someone may hear'.

There was no one nearby to listen to them because the ward was almost empty. It was the month of Mārgaśirᴏa, and the moon was shining brightly. The reflected moon rays looked like the scales of a serpent on the Henna plants planted in the hospital campus. The open ground outside seemed like a large bedsheet from which small pieces were cut and spread over the empty beds of the ward. The nurse searched for the whiskey bottle that she had kept among the medicine bottles. She was on night duty for the third time with the young doctor. They knew each other's habits and were physically close. As I was about to die in an hour, I didn't like to comment on this issue.

There was sudden darkness everywhere when I died. I could not see the nurse, the doctor, the moon, or the white bed sheet. Everything was engulfed in complete darkness as if someone had switched off the main switch of the room.

I got submerged in that darkness. The doctor was scared; he called the nurse and said that the patient had gone into a coma. The nurse stopped searching for the whiskey bottle and ran to me immediately. Suddenly he started the procedure to revive me. The doctor folded his shirt cuff and started cardiopulmonary resuscitation, and the nurse pulled out a few needles and tubes from my body and inserted a few more needles and tubes. After some time, when he couldn't revive me, he checked my pulse, checked my heartbeat, and my eyes. The nurse in open-mouthed wonderment looked at the doctor in distress. I could see her round lips and her disproportionate teeth.

I can't recollect the time when I recovered myself from that darkness. It mightn't have taken much time because as soon as I woke up, I saw the goofy teeth of the nurse and heard the doctor saying the time 'Eight fifteen.' I felt energetic after a deep long sleep, similar to the ray of sunlight after the storm. I tried to yawn and twist my fingers, but I couldn't as I had turned into weightless air.

When my mother died, I heard that the soul circles above the body at almost four feet height like a kite tied to the string in a reel after death. While taking my mother's dead body for burial, I thought the soul might get stuck on the door. The sky looked gloomy; I lent my shoulder on one side, and on the other side was my friend Madan Mohanty. Near 'Garabadu Pustakalya, a young Sikh gentleman stopped the rickshaw and bowed down in front of the dead body. I still remember a few drops of rain falling, and I looked at my mother's dead body and thought, maybe the soul was also following us. But, when I died, I understood that it was nothing like that. There was nothing called a soul. Of course, it was true that I was separated from my mortal body and had become weightless like air.

Though I had turned into weightless air, it had a shape. It had four corners, not precisely like a square but rectangular, almost equal to my body weight, like the difference in the importance of the air that we inhale and exhale. I was circling in the air of that hospital ward, not like a kite but like a sea diver who didn't require an oxygen mask. I could see my body lying on the hospital bed. I was wearing grey trousers and a red checkered shirt which the nurse and my wife made me wear after sponging my body in the morning. My thick glasses were lying on the rack next to the bed. There was no temperature anymore, so my forehead was soft and bright. I looked at my face and remembered my mother saying that my forehead was appealing. My Bengali friend's sister, Ramaa, whom I had an intimate relationship with, used to convey,' Babu Da, your lips are alluring.' During intimate moments she had held my hair tightly and bit my lips. I taught Political Science for a year in a college before joining my job. Girls occupied the first three rows in the class. Puspa, also a dancer, said facetiously, 'Sir has sharp eyes. He looks through his thick glasses, and his eyes pierce through the body.' That thick glass was now on the rack, and my eyes were closed as if I had turned into Abalakateswara.

Joganidra is a technique of closing the eyes and looking at one's body like a person who looks at the empty road from the balcony in the twinkling streetlight. My wife practiced Joganidra to maintain her mental peace whenever there was a rift between us. We regularly quarreled now, so she practiced Joganidra every afternoon and prepared herself for a quarrel at night. I had seen her in a closed room, lying down on the floor on a rug in a straight posture, covering her face with a towel, and listening to a Swamiji's instructions regarding Joganidra from a broken tape recorder. Swamiji says,' Now you move away from your body, look at your body, you can see how calm and beautiful your body is. You are the beautiful creation of God'. Of course, I never liked the obese body of my wife.

At present, without practicing Joganidra, I was away from my body. I was confined to that rectangular-shaped lightweight air that had become a part of the atmosphere. There was no effect of gravitational pull on me. I rose to the ceiling height, which was made of kadibarga, and circled the room of that old hospital ward where a fan was hanging from a long rod. I was always scared of this hanging fan during my stay in the hospital, but now I saw it closely and found that the nut and bolt of the fan had already melted and had got stuck to the iron band. It hadn't broken (only because) it belonged to the time when the British ruled.

I was now convinced about the fan. I stopped near the kadibarga ceiling, took a rest, and looked around the ward. From this height, the doctor looked much younger, and the nurse looked much shorter in stature. There was no one there, and my body wasn't entirely covered with the white bed sheet, which they usually do with a dead body. The doctor was nervous, and with a raised eyebrow, he was writing something on a paper that was kept on my bedside in that dim light. He was repeatedly saying, 'What a trouble.' The nurse also agreed to what the doctor was saying. She went closer to him and whispered in his ear, 'Today our night is ruined.' I don't know whether the doctor understood what she meant to say, but he repeated again, 'What a trouble.' They were in trouble because it was almost 10 o'clock, there was no one in the ward, the mortuary was closed, and there was no one from my house. So, to whom would they hand over the body and leave?

I thought, why should I poke my nose in this affair and left the room through the window. I could see the garbage dumped in the field in front of the medical ward - torn papers, blood-stained gauge cotton, used injection syringes, empty medicine bottles, bottle caps, and a few used condoms. Everything looked very clear in the moonlight, the wind was blowing, and a faint sound from a transistor could be heard. I was a little fatigued, so I sat on the ground for a few minutes. I remembered a few things from the past. When I was a boy, my father brought me to this hospital on his bicycle and took me to a dark room for an eye checkup to wear glasses. I was terrified. At a young age, when my mother expired in this hospital, I was sitting on this ground and smoking. I had seen a lady who looked like my mother sitting in the sun and crying. Everyone in the city knows that whoever comes to this hospital never gets cured or returns home. My father didn't come here and expired in the house. My friends and in-laws brought me to this hospital. The expression on their face was different as if they weren't taking me to the hospital but to a burial site.

I crossed the ground, and now I was on the road. I could easily walk now. I was not walking; I felt as if I was gliding. Ten days back, I was brought to the hospital in an ambulance. I wonder when I think about it. The road was almost empty; there were few rickshaws and trolley pullers lined up on the roadside to rest at night. The trolley pullers were getting ready to go to sleep, and a few rickshaw pullers were taking a rest and denying the customers to go on rental. Medicine stores and tiffin centers were spread till Mangalbagh square. Medical stores were open, and a few customers were there, but the tiffin centers had already closed by almost 11 o'clock.

I took the right turn from Mangalabagh square.

I didn't have legs; I was a four squared weightless air. I could fly at the height of a window or an electric pole or a double-storied building if I wanted. I liked Cuttack city at night. I could identify Cuttack city at night in a true sense; therefore, when I glided at the height of five feet on this empty road, I could see all the shops, the closed doors of houses, signboards, and the white mosquito net through the open window. I had reached till LIC office. Few dogs were sleeping on the road. Though I was transformed into the air, I could still feel the pinch of the cold air of December during the night as I wasn't wearing a sweater. I could see two beggars on the street burning the tire to get warmth. Two cars from the Cantonment Road side came speedily as if they were participating in a car racing competition and passed me. My shape got distorted, and I rose to my feet. I could see nearly twenty to twenty-five new white cars lined up in the Pattanaik Motors showroom. They were motionless and still like the memory. They remnded me of the white swans sleeping on a wintery morning in Lake Geneva, still and compact, covering their beak under their wings to protect themselves from cold. It seemed as if small white cushions were floating on the black water of the lake.

A few cars came from the Cantonment Road. Maybe they were returning from the club. I wouldn't take that road. I had to go to Keshu's Beetle shop to meet my friends before it closed down. I hastily walked towards Buxi Bazaar. Most of the shops were closed. A Nepali watchman with a blanket was arranging his bed on a bench on the roadside. Near Manisahu square, there was a beautiful mosque on the right-hand side. I always stood near the grill of the mosque as a child and prayed with closed eyes, and today also I did the same. I had never told about this to my mother. When I opened my eyes, I was right in front of Keshu's Betel shop.

Keshu's shop was open; it looked like a lighthouse amidst the darkness of the seashore. It would remain open because the second show wasn't yet over, and people would keep pouring out in their vehicles like bees once the show was over. Buxi Bazaar is the centre of the city. Keshu was respected by everyone, right from Akshaya Mohanty to the police constables. Police didn't dare to trouble him. He was busy rolling pan right from the evening till night with a smile on his face. There was complete darkness in the road except for the twinkling of lights, but his shop was brightly lit. I was in the hospital for the past ten days, so I hadn't eaten pan due to the restrictions in the hospital. I stood right in front of Keshu, but he couldn't see me. He again started rolling the pan. In our office, when they had asked for the address of the contact person for any emergency, I gave the address of Keshu's Beetle shop. Because I was not available at home most of the time but was present there. But today, he couldn't recognize me. This ached my heart for the first time after my death.

Why hadn't they got the news of my death even though I died four hours back? Neither Keshu nor Akshaya Bhai (who had been to Mumbai for recording), not even my three friends, Gouri, Artra, and Nati Bhai, who ordered pan, stood there and discussed something else. In the meantime, Montu came from the station side riding his bicycle. All of them greeted him by saying that;'Jagannath Express' had arrived. None of them looked at me. The clock in Keshu's shop rang. It was 12 o'clock .Suddenly there was a lot of crowd on the road as the second show got over. People stopped their scooters and bicycle and crowed over Keshu's beetle shop to purchase beetle and cigarettes. I left Buxi Bazaar and headed towards my home. Near Prabhat Cinema, I saw a newly married couple; the husband was trying to cover his young wife's head with the veil that was slipping due to the wind.

I suddenly remembered my wife and became emotional. Even today,my wife looks beautiful when she covers her head with a veil while going to the temple. She had beautiful hair when we had got married, but now she uses tassels. My wife goes to sleep by nine o'clock. She must be sleeping now with the children. Today when the beautiful nurse was sponging me in the morning, she was present and spoilt the whole game. I hated her, but I felt like seeing her once after my death. I crossed the jail, crossed the girl's school, and entered Ganga Mandir temple lane, and now it would take hardly a few minutes to reach my house. But, the road was closed as the vendors who sold mixture, boiled eggs, and golgapa had lined up with their selling carts in this narrow lane. I could see their empty selling carts and the almost sleepy eyes. I could have glided over their heads, but I had never seen this scene at night before athough I had lived in this city and died in this city, so I waited for the road to clear.

At that moment, I suddenly remembered the young doctor and the nurse in the hospital near my bed whose problem hadn't yet been solved. What would they be doing at midnight now! What else could they do near a dead body? I had become a trouble for them after my death. Their first duty was to inform about my demise to my near and dear ones but, I hadn't given them any information regarding myself. Not that I purposely did it; it happened due to circumstances. My wife, along with the children was staying at her brother's place in *Mahanadi* Vihar near Jobra as it would have been nearer to the hospital. My brother-in-law had left for Delhi by Rajdhani Express to meet his children today morning. My wife went back to our

Nimchoudi house. The doctor and the nurse tried to contact the telephone number of *Mahanadi* Vihar house, but no one picked up. They didn't know about our Nimchoudi house.

They had my cell phone number, and the doctor rang that number desperately, thinking that someone would pick up the phone, but the phone was in my pocket in vibration mode. He could hear the phone vibrating and found it in my kurta pocket. Irritated, he said,' What trouble!' The doctor suddenly remembered something. He searched his pocket and took out the visiting card of my friend Montu who had given him the card two days back when he visited the hospital. Instead of inquiring about me, he curiously asked the doctor more questions about him. Montu doesn't have a job, so he had printed the visiting card, keeping advocate as his designation. The phone number on the card wasn't valid anymore, but still, he published the same number when he reprinted the visiting card. According to him, a visiting card without a number is useless and to get the number printed is a matter of prestige. Now the doctor was trying his best to contact that number.

Presently the road was empty. Those selling carts were no more there. I proceeded towards my house. I think the Nepali guard saw me when he turned side in his sleep sleeping. No, he didn't because he turned to the other side and started snoring. I should understand that no one can see me. Our house door was closed, but I could smell the sweet fragrance of Madhumalati flowers that had bloomed outside. My mother had planted these plants when she was alive. I crossed the boundary wall and entered the courtyard. There was silence everywhere, and I could see our pet dog Miki sleeping there. He guarded the house, and if he barked, then everyone would get up. Miki looked at me; he recognized me and came near and then went back to sleep silently. I placed my hand on his head, and he liked my delicate fingers. I recalled the story of Ulysses when he returned to Ithaca; neither his wife Penelope nor anybody else could recognize him except his dog.

I entered the house and saw my wife sleeping with both of the children on either side. My daughter slept with her back turned, but my son was sleeping his face buried in her bosom just like I had done for a few years after our marriage. There was no place for a husband here. They were all sleeping so peacefully that they had no way of knowing that I was already dead. They would come to know after visiting the hospital tomorrow morning. I took the telephone receiver and kept it aside, thinking that the doctor may get the telephone number from somewhere and give a call. It was almost 2 a.m., and I had very little time in my hand to arrange a few of my things for the last time.

When I say my things, I mean some proof regarding my infidelity which I had tried my best to keep as a secret from the menancing eyes of my wife. Children had grown up now, so I needed to be more careful. I looked at the bed; three of them were sleeping very innocently. Even in their dreams, they could have never imagined the thunder that would strike the tragedy that would befall them next day morning. They would cry, mourn, and take me to perform the last rites. I worked in a private office, so I didn't know if my wife would get a job in the office or not. I wasn't an ideal employee. They wouldn't stay in this house. Maybe my wife would go back to her maternal home in *Mahanadi* Vihar, and my children, after growing up, might go to Delhi or Hyderabad for further studies and stay in a hostel. These would happen later, but the main problem would arise when they would take my belongings from this house.

I left the bedroom and went back to my room. Before marriage and even after marriage, I had a room of my own with my books, a few music cassettes, and a single bed. The room had restricted entry. There was a black and white photograph of mine fr my BA days hanging on the wall. I stood in front of the picture and remembered that when Sulekha saw me for the first time in my third year, I looked exactly like how I looked in the photograph. I didn't have a single photograph of Sulekha, but I had a bundle of sixty-seven letters that she wrote to me in our three years of courtship. We got drifted apart nearly twenty-seven years back. Sulekha got married and went to Singapore and then to Australia. I never saw her after that. I knew that somewhere there still remained the scarf which she had left one day in this house. It was now tied to the bunch of letters. Initially I used to read her letters every day, but they have remained untouched for the last fifteen years. It remained in my heart just like my breath.

Two days before my marriage, I made a bundle of these letters and handed them to my mother. My mother understood my feelings, but she didn't utter a single word. She took the bundle and kept it in a wooden box underneath the winter clothes. My wife hardly took out any winter clothes from that wooden box as it wasn't very cool in this city during winter. So she could never get them. After my mother's death, I quietly took out those letters from the wooden box and hid them in the last rack of the iron cupboard behind the books in my private room. But, where would I take those letters today?

There were so many things left with me that belonged to Sulekha and others. After I became mature, I met many people in different stages of my life, shaped new relationships, and those relationships faded with time. I destroyed many such proofs in the office incinerator, but I couldn't beat this, which was related to Sulekha. It was the most precious relationship among all the relationships. It was always there in my consciousness.

Next to the iron cupboard, there was an old, broken chest of drawers made up of a Bhutan board. I switched on the lights and pulled the last drawer, which was a little challenging to open. I kept many things very carefully in that drawer under the ragged clothes. There was a plastic wheel, which Ela had given to me when I was in the ninth standard. When blown, the words 'I Love You' written inside it became visible. There was also a safety pin. Before attending college, during summer vacation, Chhabi was annoyed with me, and she chewed the safety pin and bent it; I kept it. She got married to an Army Major and became a widow. When she narrated this incident to her husband on their first night, the Major took it lightly and smoked a cigarette. I kept the green broken bangles of Sabita in a diary, few foreign stamps, a stopwatch which wasn't working, a knife made up of white bone, half-used lipstick of Binita Boudi, photographs of two girls which had come for matchmaking purposes, the perfume bottle that was my first gift to Rita (she returned it in anger) ,a twenty years old Marcopolo cigarette packet which Jill Westkirt, the vagabond hippie had left in Puri, friendship bands, red ribbon, and the tie pin. What would I do with these things?

I returned to the courtyard with a lot of anxiety. It was almost time for daybreak, the smell of Madhumalati flowers was more pungent, and Miki looked at me, smiled, and wagged his tail. I didn't know whether dogs could smile or not, but Miki smiled. I went to the bedroom and saw the three sleeping peacefully without any movement. I returned to the courtyard feeling a little tense and thought, whatever I wanted to do, I should do it immediately as there wasn't much time left. If they found Sulekha's letter, my wife and my family would lose the faith they had in me.

There were sixty-seven letters written over three years. Some were written on inland letters, and most were sent in the envelopes. The salutation had first started formally and gradually ended up in an informal manner. The contents included the Bali Yatra visit, the annoyance of not meeting during the summer vacation, our dream of getting married, having children, naming them, and a few things related to our breakup. Others mocked me for these letters. Once my younger sister brought a letter from the post-man, kept it in front of me and left without saying anything. Another time Akshaya Bhai snatched a letter from me and read it loudly in Buxi Bazaar. I was embarrassed. What would I do now?

I should tear those letters and then burn them. Where was the match stick? I saw a lighter in the drawer. I don't know if it would get ignited or not. Otherwise, I would flush it in the toilet.No; I should burn it. These were worth getting burnt in the sacred fire like my dead body would burn tomorrow. I would take these letters and along with everything kept in my diary with me. But, How? I would take it in a bag, but I didn't have my hands. If I didn't have hands, then how did the drawer open? How were the letters kept behind the books on the chest of drawers?

It was true!Really! Sulekha's letters tied in a blue polka dot scarf were waiting for me. Suddenly I felt the warmth. I kept placed my palm on them caressing them, put it back in the iron cupboard's last rack behind the books, and closed the cabinet. I pushed the old drawer and closed it, and in it hid a few precious things beneath the ragged clothes.

I came outside. It was almost time for sunrise, and

I could see the blue sky. The northern star was glowing. I had to go. How could I deny the life I have ((had) led for so many years? My life was an amalgamation of sweet memories and bad dreams. What should I take, and what should I leave behind? Could I take the sweet fragrance of *Madhumalati* flowers with me? During my college days, the image of Sulekha, draped in a blue saree would enter my imagination along with the sweet smell of these flowers in the wee hours. I have tried to conceal my secrets like a coward when I was alive to avoid disgrace. Would I defame myself after my death destroying these? Let things be there. How much could I change this world, and why should I?

STORY 11

The Tale of a Southern City

I had spent my childhood and eleven years of schooling in this southern coastal city. I visited the town almost after thirty years, just for a day, and all the memories attached to this city were again resuscitated. My father worked in the Central Post office and was posted in different places all over the country, but I have spent a significant part of my life in this city. We lived in a bungalow next to the office of the main Post office. My elder brother broke his leg in this city and was under traction for three months, my father got his promotion twice, my old grandmother expired, my younger sister was born, and I finished my schooling from here and left for Delhi for my higher studies. Today, after thirty years, while traveling in a cab (the city doesn't have an airport or any star hotels till now) from the station to the hotel, I could feel that the city hasn't (hadn't) changed much, although it seemed to be a little unknown to me.

Nowadays in our country, trains arrive according to their scheduled time. My train arrived early in the morning at five-thirty. It was almost bright. The cab driver was standing with a placard in his hand. While walking towards the cab, I looked at the sky. The sky was clear and blue; the moisture in the air made me nostalgic. I thanked God that, at least for a day, I was away from the hazy, smoke-filled, grey sky of Delhi.

The program had been arranged in the hotel conference room where I was staying. The program assessed a few NGOs' works and gave a contract to the best NGO for three years. A nationwide stir on judicial reforms had began, and few International organizations were involved. I had come to this selection committee program as an advisor to an International organization. The fraternity of the International organizations would fetch an excellent grant to the selected NGO. While going through the details kept in the reception, I realized that there were six NGOs who would give their presentation for the grant in the morning. It would be followed by lunch and the closing. There were five people in the selection committee, out of which three were from the South, whom I didn't know, and the fourth one was from Delhi like me, and his name was Ajay Dua. He was my college friend, and at present, he holds (held) the post of Additional Secretary in the Department of Commerce.

The session began in the afternoon. It started with the presentation of the incredible work in this field, followed by a few question-answer sessions. Two to three representatives were invited for discussion from each organization, and secrecy was maintained. Our topic of discussion was more regarding the commercial sector rather than judicial reform. We discussed the necessary resources for the project and the International export taxes analysis. As it was a global tender, an organization from Sri Lanka had participated in the bidding. There was also a lot of argument between two Indian NGOs and the consultants of an International Law farm. on the topic 'Common Law'.

Our meeting had started precisely at 9 a.m. After a rigorous discussion of three hours with the NGOs, we took a coffee break for coffee. There was a state of uneasiness.

No one was fit to be selected. The crucial aspect of this project was forgotten because of the arguments, which were totally out of context. Though we maintained secrecy still, the proposal of each NGO was similar. Finally, Ajay Dua shouted, 'What the hell!' and left the room in discontentment to smoke.

After he returned, the meeting resumed. The organization which came forward couldn't convince us, and we couldn't select them. They left, and as we weren't satisfied, we gave a second thought to float a tender again. It was almost noon, and there was still one NGO that was yet to come with its proposal. When the two representatives of the NGOs entered the room to explain their proposal, we didn't expect anything more from them.

Out of the six NGOs selected forbidding, this was the only local organization. Though they worked in Trichi and Coimbatore, their head office was in the same city. One of the representatives was a solid and stout aged person who was shabbily dressed in a white trouser and black coat like an advocate, and a simple, dark-skinned girl accompanied him. The girl was draped in a white saree with a black border, and she looked more like a nun than an advocate. She looked like a junior assistant of this aged gentleman.

The gentleman started talking, but it was difficult to comprehend the subject matter because of his rough voice. It took time for us to understand that he was actually speaking in English rather than in any other South Indian language. When he started giving the presentation and his comments, the girl could know that all his efforts were in vain. She immediately came to us and handed over a typed paper on which there was a brief summary of what the man was speaking. It was indeed an intelligent act. When she came closer, I noticed that she was tall, had deep dark eyes, and her skin was as smooth as black marble. No matter how plain she looked from afar, seen at close quarter, her attractiveness was noticeable.

The gentleman abruptly ended his speech when he saw us not paying attention to him. Whatever he said after that, was the most unintentitional. Ajay Dua shrugged his shoulders again said,'What the hell'? And when he was about to leave the place, the girl said,' Excuse me, Sir. Please wait, I'll explain. The senior representative held his ground, sat down on the chair, and nodded his head as a sign of approval.

The girl spoke for nearly ten minutes. While saying ((speaking) there was a change in her personality. She spoke fluently and in an impressive way. The way she justified her points impressed us, and we couldn't contradict her.

In brief, she explained to us that the project we wanted to begin to was itself opposed by the court and the lawyers.

The vicious circle they have created for years, being parochial and self-centered, wasn't easy to break using computers and softwares. It would all go in vain. She said the International scholar who was quite knowledgeable about 'Common Law' didn't have any experience regarding the social aspects of this country. Jurisdiction originates from tradition and culture; therefore, if imposed, this teaching project wouldn't be fruitful until it was implemented and accepted at the grassroots level by the ordinary clients, among advocates and court employees.

After concluding her justifications, this intelligent girl didn't sit down but walked towards us confidently as if she wanted an explanation. In the meantime, the ordinary and trivial appearance had transformed into brilliance and astute. She caressed the wavy hair on her forehead with contentment.

All of us wanted to say something or the other. I stood up, smiled, stood up smilingly, wished her, and said that we were in a dilemma right from the beginning of the day, and her clear and concise presentation had emanated hope. We were sure that quickly, we would come up with a solution. After they left, we had an internal discussion, and except Ajay Dua, the rest of us recommended this NGO to be appointed. Ajay wasn't happy with this decision and said that if we do this, we might be accused of populism. He charged me and said that I should not have indirectly announced the results before the voting process had begun.

Almost half of them had left by lunch time, and few didn't come. The banquet hall had tint glasses, so it was dark. Ajay Dua was having a beer in the bar stall. The girl who had suddenly become the focus of attention was standing alone and was having her lunch in a corner. I didn't go to her; I searched for her solid and stout senior but couldn't find him. An accountant came and took my signature on a paper regarding TA and DA at that moment. After he left, I saw that the girl wasn't there in the hall anymore. I was a little embarrassed and walked towards the reception. I could see the girl there, but before I could say hello, she opened the door and left.

I left the hall after she. Under the open sky at noon, the scorching heat was unbearable, but the moisture-laden air from the sea gave relief. A small road right from the front of the hotel intersected with the main road. We both were walking alone on that road. She might have seen me, maybe because of the sound made by my footsteps or perhaps because she turned back. Yet I wasn't so close to her to read the expression on her face. I wasn't close enough to read the expression on her face.

There was no one on that small road; though I was far from her, I still felt near close to her. Although we were walking shoulder to shoulder, there was no closeness between us, and I couldn't speak to her because of the crowd and commotion on the main road . But I could now make out that she was pretty older in age much older which I wasn't able to make out out in the dim light of the hotel before. Her white saree reflected the sun's rays. She wasn't dark but had a deep bronze color complexion. She didn't look so attractive from near.

Sometimes we walked in the middle of the road and sometimes on the left side. I thought of speaking to her, but I couldn't as the road was overcrowded. Suddenly a bus came from behind and blew the horn, she moved towards the left side, and I was in the middle of the road. After the bus left, I saw her at a distance; she was walking along with a hermit with a white beard and hair. The man was lean and thin, wore a torn saffron shirt, rudraksha beads adorned his neck, a tilak on his forehead, and smoked a cigarette. I couldn't hear what they were talking about as it was very noisy.

We walked for some time. Many shops were closed as it was afternoon. I couldn't read what was written on the signboard as I didn't know the language. After walking for quite some time, suddenly they entered a lane on the right-hand side. While entering the road, she slightly turned to confirm whether I was still following her or not. I felt as if she gave me an unclear invitation through her look.

Charmed by her look, I also entered the lane.

After leaving the main road, the route gradually became narrower. The road was untidy. There were drains on both sides of the street. The road had potholes that were filled with smashed bricks. Both sides of the road were dumped with garbage. Finally, we reached a house made up of brick that wasn't cemented. The old door of the house had a Swastik sign drawn with vermillion. The door was looking shabby because of the oil and ghee stains. A red and yellow color flag was fluttering at the top of the house like a flag on a temple like that of a temple. The place looked like a temporary or half-constructed temple. So, the person with grey hair wasn't a hermit but a priest of this temple.

It was all dark inside, but I could see the rangoli drawn on the floor when I opened the door and peeped inside. A lamp was burning very dimly in front of the idol and pictures of God. The girl, through her eyes indicated me to enter the room. I kept my shoes out and went inside. After entering the room, the priest left the room with a very satisfied look. As soon as he left, the girl closed the door, and the room was pitch dark once more.

I am one of those who can't see anything when it suddenly becomes dark. I usually pause for a few minutes whenever I enter the cinema hall. I was anxious to know about the girl from since the morning, and the darkroom, which seemed like a dark cave, triggered my anxiety. I couldn't see her but could only hear the jingling anklet sound of the girl and could make out that she was moving towards the interior, leaving the room.

I followed the girl in the darkness and came across a door with a wire mesh on the other side of the wall. I went through a gate and reached a place that wasn't a room; it was a narrow porch. An asbestos roof covered the patio, which was very low in height, and towards the end of the porch, there was a grill made from thin bamboo strips that through which entered the light, forming a triangle. A petticoat, a few undergarments, and a colorful saree were spread out on the railing of the grill for drying. I could see a little bit of the exterior through the grill. There were vegetables planted in a row, a corn farm, and a netted fence. At a distance, I could see the cattle grazing. When I looked at the sky from there, I could make out a sea nearby.

It was dark inside. There were few things kept on that narrow porch, like a chair, a book rack, a jug on a small stool, and a broken table. There was a single bed made up of wooden planks covered with a bedsheet and a white pillow. A few broken wood and iron objects were there on one side of the porch. There were two or three large vessels, a few spatulas, and a table fan that wasn't working. There was a stove and a few utensils for cooking on the other side. There was a cloth stand on which clothes were folded and kept in the corner. There was a small mirror on the outside wall on which one could see the image in a standing position. There were a few small and big black sticker bindis stuck to the mirror. Did the girl stay here? and if she did, was she permanently staying there or occasionally, I couldn't say.

I was sweating as it was hot and humid. At that moment, the girl indicated me to sit down on the bed. She also sat down in the corner. In that darkness, I kept my hand on her hand. It was warm, and she didn't take it back. I asked her, 'What's your name?' She answered after some time,' Surya Kumari.'I looked into her eyes, and she looked down. I looked at her bare shoulder and was excited. The sun rays falling through the grill reflected and created a triangular pattern on her body.

On that shadowed porch, as I held her close in my arms, we both were sweating. The bed made a creaking sound. Her conscious body responded and bent like an arch. It went for a long time, and we both were exhausted. At that moment of tranquility, I saw the color of her nipples. It was similar to her lips, like a half-burnt metal.

She was still lying on the bed when I left her and covered her chest with the half-open saree. I didn't feel that conscious when I crossed the room where the Gods were kept but became conscious when I saw that hermit leaning on the broken wall and smoking. I felt as if he was waiting for me to go outside. I came to the main road; it was evening, the shops were open, and I could feel the cool breeze blowing.

In the evening I went to the local club. I had spent eleven years of my adolescent age in this place, but at present, I didn't have many friends in this city. As I had informed them beforehand, a few of them had come. They have done different types of jobs, and I used to see them when they went to Delhi. By the time I reached the club, they were almost drunk.

I was deeply engrossed in the thoughts of' Surya Kumari. I asked,' Does anyone know Surya Kumari?' One of them asked, 'Who is she?' The other one said,' I know.' The third one asked,' How do you know?'. ' This is a small city, brother!' said my fourth friend. The fifth one questioned, 'How do you know her?' I narrated the incident that happened in the morning. Bikas, a doctor, immediately recognized her and said she was a good lady. She belonged to Nagercoil and was a Christian. She was a lawyer and has done her LLB. Nagendra Swami, a lawyer, said, 'She is a useless lawyer. What does she know about the law? Stupid lady! She is only seen with Krishna Kumar.' 'Which Krishna Kumar?' Bikas asked. In a very firm voice, Nagendra Swami said, the fat man who was the president of the Bar Association. He had kept this lady, and his family's life was wholly spoilt because of this lady.

Raghav, who works for the local newspaper, twisted the episode. He said Krishna Kumar had already left Surya Kumari. Maybe he visited her sometimes. Nowadays, she cooked food in a temple and supplied it to different offices in the lunch box. Nagendra Swami again said,' In this city, she is well known amongst the ones who are forced bachelors or who are away from home and staying without their wives. They look for her every time.' Nagen was drunk and fould mouthed.

I asked Raghav,' Who is that hermit'? Raghav said,' Oh! He is the priest in that temple and also a cook. He has given her a place to stay. God knows! What is there between them? A few of them say that he is her father-in-law and she eloped with him, but I don't believe in rumors'.Nagen came to me and said,' If you want to know about Surya Kumari, ask Govind Rao. He is her doctor. No one drinks like her in this city. He has been treating her for fifteen years as she suffers from Dipsomania'. He also added that her son was almost fourteen years old . He looked like Govind. Govind had kept him in a boarding school in Waltair.

Govind was a known Psychotherapist in Southern India. He had earned a lot. Nagendra Swami was damn stupid, and Govind was damn clever. He laughed from a distance and said,' Nagen is a rascal. Don't listen to him. He can write a script for AVM and produce a film'. Govind took advantage of the young ladies on the pretext of psychological treatment, and everyone knew that despite his excellent reputation as a doctor. Govind had never seen a film in the last fifteen years and didn't know that AVM didn't produce films nowadays. Govind came closer and said,'Surya Kumari has left drinking long back, and I have stopped giving her medicine. She was drinking as she wasn't getting good sleep. Now, if she doesn't get the rest, I tell her a story to make her sleep'. There was a mockery in his statement as he laughed.

That night I could hardly get a wink of sleep in the air-conditioned coupe of that train. I wondered if Surya Kumari too is similarly battling with sleep on the wooden plank of that gloomy alley, where in the afternoon, she had ungrudgingly submitted to my lust, as if it was a part of her siesta. Suddenly I was overcome by a deep grimace, and as is my wont, I made a commitment of life long relationship with Surya kumari in that running train, though I knew quite well that the possibility of meeting her again is as good as none.

□□

Postscript to 5 Ways to Kill Ramaa

Willy and obstreperous girls have always held my fascination no matter how much oddities we may have to compromise with. The queer and louder they are, they press the throttle of my adrenalin chamber harder. Bursts of dopamine flood my cerebram like stardust. Rama is one such young misadventure, who tortures her love lorn protagonist so much that he is left with no option but to plan her homicide. Rama on the other hand is ready to die happily in the excess of love. It is a story of reverse osmosis told in the language of accute passion and deep longing.

Devdas Chhotray